DEATH IN THE SCILLIES

What had happened to the expert yachtsman, whose unmanned boat had drifted on to the Seven Sisters Reef? After two months his body has not been found and Martin Yates, an ex-marine brought up in the Scillies, is called in to solve the mystery. Yates learns that a doubtful character is recruiting a bodyguard for a millionaire socialite and also that both had stayed at the same hotel as the missing man. What is the connection—and why should bodyguards be needed in the Scillies, one of the most peaceful corners of the earth?

HOWARD CHARLES DAVIS

DEATH IN THE SCILLIES

Complete and Unabridged

LINFORD
Leicester

First published in Great Britain in 1968

First Linford Edition
published May 1989

British Library CIP Data

Davis, Howard Charles
Death in the Scillies.—Large print ed.—
Linford mystery library
I. Title
823′.914[F]

ISBN 0-7089-6725-6

Published by
F. A. Thorpe (Publishing) Ltd.
Anstey, Leicestershire
Set by Rowland Phototypesetting Ltd.
Bury St. Edmunds, Suffolk
Printed and bound in Great Britain by
T. J. Press (Padstow) Ltd., Padstow, Cornwall

1

CHARLES EVERARD was the last person I expected to hear from when I went in to the Services Club one June morning. Increasing poverty had long ago made me think of giving up my membership for the few guineas it cost me. But it had its uses. The club was a useful postal address for a man who was always dodging around, and it provided an ex-Marine like me, who had nothing in particular to recommend him, with a number of useful contacts when it came to looking for a job. I was hoping to see a man named Stannard, who had once hinted that he could put a job my way.

I didn't see Stannard, but I had been in the coffee room a bare three minutes, since it was too early for a drink, when I found old Ponting at my elbow. Ponting is the club's porter and older than the oldest member. Protocol and the courtesies of the old world are his gods.

"Begging your pardon, sir, Major Everard left a message for you when he was in to dinner

1

last night. His compliments, sir, and will you be good enough to telephone him at this number?"

Ponting presented me with a piece of paper on which the number had been written in a flowing and impeccable script, and bowed himself off.

Charles Everard had been my OC at one time. We had both left the service in roughly the same month of the same year, and I recalled that he had gone into some hush-hush department of the Metropolitan Police. He had even suggested that I join him, but if I had it wouldn't have been on his level and the idea had not appealed to me. I was sure that his request to telephone him was not a repeat of the offer, and I was puzzled. I had taken a few jobs since leaving the Marines, and in one of them I had found my employer to be an out-and-out crook, but apart from that brief interlude I had kept my nose reasonably clean. So what did he want?

I went out to the box in the hall, dialled the number and plugged in my sixpence as soon as it began to pip. I didn't get Everard, only a female voice that passed me on to another voice, male this time but still not Everard. However, I left the box with a request to call at three o'clock that afternoon at an address in Queen's Gate.

I arrived on the dot. It was raining buckets and I was glad to duck in out of the wet having walked from Knightsbridge.

A commissionaire checked me against a list.

"Room forty, sir. Fourth floor."

An ancient lift carried me creakily upwards and deposited me in a corridor painted pea-green. I was right opposite a door marked 40, so I knocked and was told to go in. There was a girl in it seated at a typewriter. If she was Everard's secretary, which I supposed her to be, then there was something to be said for a job in the police. She was a knock-out. Blonde hair, dark brown eyes full of camaraderie, and a figure that made a mini-skirt a danger to the male population.

"Martin Yates to see Major Everard," I grinned.

"Go right in, Captain Yates. You're expected. Isn't it ghastly weather?" she added, seeing my rain-soaked shoulders and hat.

"Brighter now," I said, and she returned her eyes to her typewriter rather hastily.

Charles Everard was in his early forties and

greying at the temples, but put him in battle-dress and he would still look the natural leader of a landing party, ready for anything. I had always liked him. He came from a family who for generations had served their country for precious little in the way of rewards. There seem to be fewer and fewer of his type coming out of the mould in these modern times.

"Sit down, Martin," he invited, after we had shaken hands and exchanged the usual courtesies. "It's good of you to come. I won't waste time. Tell me, you're a Scillonian, aren't you? Born in St. Mary's?"

"That's not exactly right, Charles. I wasn't born there. I know the Scillies well. I had an uncle, my mother's brother, who owned a farm on the east side above Pelistry Bay. I used to spend all my summer holidays there as a boy, right up to my late teens. Uncle Horace, I'm sorry to say, is now extinct, and the farm is not even in the family. Happy days," I sighed. "Why do you want to know?"

"It's about Raymond Sikes," he said.

"Who?" I demanded.

"Colonel Sikes. Surely you remember him?"

"Oh, 'Bill' Sikes. Yes, of course I do."

"Then you must have read of his supposed

4

death in a yachting accident in the Scillies towards the end of April?"

I stared at him.

"That was Colonel Sikes? Heaven help me, Charles, I never knew it. Of course I read of it, but I never connected it with our Sikes. He was inevitably known as 'Bill', and no one ever called him anything but Bill."

He nodded.

"Well, I'm one of his executors if he's dead, and I think he is, though it may be years before we can get the courts to declare it, and seeing his full name so many times lately probably made me use it. So you're familiar with what happened?"

"With what was reported as having happened," I corrected him.

He smiled and pushed a box of cigarettes across his desk towards me. I helped myself and lit up.

"I can tell you that what was reported is pretty well *all* that is known to have happened. More's the pity." He leant back in his chair. "As you probably know, Bill Sikes was a keen yachtsman. He sailed alone. He had a twenty-footer, schooner-rigged, which he could handle himself with ease. On the night of the 28th

5

April last, when there was a full moon and a fair breeze, he left the harbour in Hugh Town, St. Mary's, intent as far as we know on a sail round the islands . . ."

"A trifle early in the season," I put in.

Everard shrugged.

"Perhaps. The first full moon of the season, anyway. That may have prompted the trip. The night was warm . . ."

"Yes, I was forgetting he was in the Scillies. They seldom ever have a frost. Sorry, Charles. Please go on."

"You had a point there, even so," he pointed out. "It was not warm enough for Sikes to be living on his yacht. He was staying at Delgardens Hotel, but I'll come back to that in a moment. He was seen out in the Road soon after leaving harbour by another yachtsman, a man named Reeves-Galway, who was fishing. Incidentally, he also was a guest in Delgardens, pending the final touches to a house he's had built on St. Mary's. At dawn the next morning Sikes' yacht, the *Globe*, drifted on to the Seven Sisters Reef. She was spotted by the crew of the lightship there, and they fired rockets to warn him off as they thought. They also radioed for the St. Mary's lifeboat, but by the time she got

6

there the *Globe* had broken up; even the dinghy he'd been towing astern. All the same, there was not much doubt that Sikes was not aboard when she went on the rocks."

"Sounds as if his course was north when last seen," I suggested.

"It was," he concurred, and leant forward to rummage in a drawer of his desk. "I've a map of the Scillies here . . ."

"I don't need it, Charles. His course would have taken him slap into St. Martin's, so he must have gone out through Crow Sound have altered course to the east. Of course, in a small yacht and on a full tide he could have gone out between St. Martin's and the Eastern Isles, or even bore off westwards and then got out to the open sea through Tean Sound, or piddled around between Tresco and St. Martin's and then through the Beef Neck, but whatever happened to him he must have been clear of the Islands before he went overboard or the yacht would have fetched up in the Islands. Has there been an enquiry?"

"Yes, she was registered and insured at Lloyd's. I can give you a transcription of the proceedings such as they were. He was presumed to have gone overboard in some

7

mysterious accident not wearing a life-jacket and been lost. His body has not been found."

"Charles," I said carefully, "accidents do happen even to the most experienced yachtsmen, but you obviously don't believe it. Why not?"

He tapped the long ash off the end of his cigarette.

"In the first place I was sceptical because I knew Bill Sikes well. He was a man who excelled at most things, and he was a careful man, Martin. He always wore a life-jacket at sea and he would have worn one then, certainly on a trip taking him clear of the Islands into the Atlantic. I just could not see him going overboard in a moderate sea, and that made me go into the circumstances a little more closely than normally I would have done. I ought to explain," he went on, stirring restlessly in his chair, "that my interest is purely a private one. As far as the police are concerned, and really there is precious little for them to be concerned with, the man in charge is Superintendent Trevillian of the Cornish Constabulary in Penzance."

I nodded.

"But you want my help?"

"If you can give it. I simply cannot find the time, and what suspicions I have at the moment are not strong enough to warrant official action."

"Suspicions of what?" I asked quickly. "Dirty work?"

"Possibly. I might add that I have used my official position to strengthen suspicion."

I thought for a moment or two, while his grey eyes studied me seriously.

"Charles," I said, "I would like to help, especially if it means a trip to the Scillies. They are only twenty minutes in a helicopter from Penzance these days but for me over the past four or five years they could have been a million miles away. I'm poorer than a parson's pig. You must know that?"

"I do, Martin, and I'm sorry . . ."

"Then why ask me? Agreed, I know the Scillies . . ." I broke off as the penny dropped. He was a policeman. "Listen, Charles," I said, "have you another reason?"

"I have," he smiled, "and you'll know what it is in a moment. You must understand, Martin, that I had nothing but the bare facts I've related to go on. Even the enquiry has brought out no more, except possibly the

9

evidence of the Coastguard Station on St. Mary's who logged him passing north down the Road and then lost interest in him . . ."

"I was wondering about the Coastguard," I put in. "They wouldn't worry overmuch about a local yachtsman."

"Nor did they," Everard said. "It might have been useful if they had. However, if Sikes had not been lost by accident then I had to assume an alternative. It is inconceivable that he staged his own disappearance. He was moderately wealthy, a bachelor who enjoyed life, and fit as a fighting cock; physically a very young forty-four-year-old. What else? Murder? Possibly. If it was it was premeditated. I'm sure nobody boarded him on the off chance of his carrying a lot of cash with him. Suicide? Ridiculous. It left me with premeditated murder."

"Motive?" I asked.

"That remains to be found, but an apparent lack of motive doesn't rule out murder."

Everard stubbed out his cigarette.

"I had his fellow guests at the hotel investigated. It was early in the season. Normally they don't open till May, but Reeves-Galway, the man who was out fishing that night, is a millionaire, had needed accommodation during April

while his house was finished and persuaded them to open up. So they took in any others who came along. There were half a dozen. All spotless of character, Martin, save one couple, a Mr. and Mrs. John Cookson."

"Cookson?" I cried. "You must be joking! What the hell was he doing there? Ye gods! I get it now, Charles. I worked for Cookson for a spell as a sort of private eye."

I waited for him to laugh, but he didn't. He looked at me with his eyes disconcertingly grave.

"Go on, please, Martin. We know that Cookson runs the Belsize Detective Agency. It handles a great deal of divorce work. Indeed few of the two thousand private detectives in this country do little else. It's lucrative."

"Very," I agreed, "but I was green. I answered his advertisement. I don't know what I imagined the work was, but I found that trailing erring husbands was not my cup of tea. However, I stuck it for a mounth or two, then turned it in because I had a shrewd idea that Cookie, as everyone called him, was not above blackmailing the guilty party when he saw the way clear."

"How do you know that?"

"For one thing he equipped his operatives with buttonhole cameras which to my mind was unnecessary. The idea was you caught the guilty parties *in flagrante delecto*, warned them and then gave evidence in court. For another, one of his clients happened to be a woman I knew slightly. I met her quite by chance leaving the office as I was going in. She told me that she was disappointed no progress was being made in her case. I was under the impression that much progress had been made. I tackled Cookson on the subject. He denied it, of course. We called each other a few choice names, exchanged threats of violence, and I told him what he could do with his work. I was looking for an excuse to turn in a job I loathed, anyway."

Everard said:

"Thank you, Martin. It is something we have long suspected of Cookson, but as you can imagine that sort of thing is very difficult to pin down and bring to court. We also know him, though he has never been convicted, as a con man, as a very clever fence, and indeed capable of doing anything which will bring him in what is known colloquially as a fast buck."

He paused, and smiled.

"All that, however, has nothing whatsoever to do with Bill Sikes. Cookson can take a holiday in the Scillies along with his wife . . ."

"Gloria," I supplied. "She works as his secretary and is as bent as her husband."

"No doubt," Everard agreed. "But the fact remains of all the half-dozen guests in the hotel only the Cooksons can be said to be in any way doubtful in character. Not much to go on, is it?"

"Damn all, if you ask me."

"So," he went on, "I had to probe farther, even to the juxtaposition of the various guests' rooms. No help there. The Cooksons were sandwiched between an eminent barrister and a church deacon. Bill Sikes had a smaller room on another floor, and Reeves-Galway, who does things on a grand scale, had taken three rooms, one of which had been turned into a lounge."

"If Cookson was there with a purpose," I pointed out, "The situation of his room wouldn't worry him overmuch. He would have gone well equipped for eavesdropping. I know for a fact, that he possesses radio bugs. They're illegal, but . . ." I shrugged my shoulders. "What sort of person is Reeves-Galway, the millionaire?" I asked. "Cookie may have gone there considering him as a pigeon ripe for plucking."

Everard chuckled.

"A somewhat difficult pigeon, Martin. Reeves-Galway is a typical rich socialite. His father built up the big Midlands Engineering Group and left him a packet. Reeves-Galway is thirty-seven years old. He has been married three times, and his present wife was an Italian film actress. He doesn't seem to be able to sire children. His second wife, who died a natural death—the first one was divorced—persuaded him to adopt a son. The boy is now seven years old . . ."

"You've certainly done a job of probing, Charles," I interrupted, "but what on earth can the histories of these people have to do with Bill Sikes' death?"

"I wish I knew," he admitted calmly, "but I've cast my net wide hoping some useful scrap will come in. I was going to point out," he went on, "that Reeves-Galway would be a difficult subject to fleece. He's done most things in his time. Motor racing, ocean racing, polo, flying. You name it, Reeves-Galway has played it. He's tough, Martin. A playboy but no push-over. He has only one peculiarity. He loathes publicity.

14

People such as he come in for a lot of it, but Reeves Galway goes out of his way to avoid it. He has bought his way out of the society weeklies and the gossip columns."

"Did Sikes know him?"

"They met at the hotel."

"Cripes, Charles!" I protested, "it's all so thin, gossamer thin. A small group in an hotel opened earlier in the season than usual. Sikes probably met the lot. What do you want me to do, Charles, that can't be done by the local CID?"

"I'm coming to that," he answered, paused, and then went on:

"Martin, would you say that the Scillies were unlikely to be the scene of any crime?"

"Of course. The Scillonians are the most friendly and law-abiding folk on earth. But any crook can visit them along with honest men."

"Exactly. Towards the end of last year, Martin, a body that had been in the water for three months was washed up on the Breton coast. Interpol circulated photographs of it to member countries. What remained of the clothing had been identified as of English make, so we paid the photographs particular attention. A peculiar tattoo mark on the right forearm had

15

been treated to a close-up by the photographer and so had the legs. There were no feet but the legs showed signs of having been bound. The torso had wounds suggesting the man had died from stabbing. You follow me?"

"All the way. The body had been weighted at the feet and dumped in deep water."

"We think so," Everard agreed. "I ought to tell you," he went on, "that this was a fluke of memory on my part. I was casting around for a record of any crime remotely connected with the Scillies. I was sure that I'd read or heard some mention of them during the past few months. I delved into records and this incident came to light. Oddly enough the tattoo mark was remembered by a man on our staff who claimed that a London policeman, by name Albert Henry Blagdon and a man who had been slung out of the force for taking graft, had carried the same tattoo mark on his right forearm. Efforts to trace Blagdon, who had not been reported missing, were made. His last known movements under his own name were not in the Scillies but in Penzance where he stayed a night last June in a pub, and made no secret of the fact that he was going to St. Mary's on the next morning's boat. The experts agree

16

that a body dumped off the Scillies might well fetch up on the Breton coast."

"So what?" I demanded and added hastily, "Sorry, Charles, but . . ."

"Let me finish, Martin. You're always too quick off the mark. I had Blagdon's history investigated. As you can imagine it was not a good one. At one time, like you, he worked for the Belsize Detective Agency. Cookson employed him as a part-time operative. The tattoo mark was not a definite identification. Tattoists usually present would be clients with a selection of their art, and more than one client can select the same design. But if it *was* Blagdon then obviously I had to turn my attention to last year. I did. I learnt that Cookson, Reeves-Galway, and the Archdeacon, who I am sure is innocent, were all on St. Mary's at the same time last year."

"I can see the possibilities," I admitted, "but I still can't think where I fit in."

Everard opened a drawer in his desk, and pulled out a newspaper already folded, which he pushed towards me.

"Cookson is advertising for staff," he said, and added, "At least one assumes as much though he calls it very special duties for which

17

only men of the right educational background and with high physical qualities need apply. This ad first appeared a week ago, and is still running. What about it Martin? I want you to apply for re-employment with Cookson. I'm sure that he knows something of Sikes' death. You know why I'm asking you; why I can't send one of my own men. Will you do it?"

18

2

IN vain I pointed out to Everard that Cookson, after the way he and I had parted brass rags would be the last person to want to re-employ me.

"I'm not so sure, Martin," he returned equably. "I think you underestimate your own capabilities. You've had experience of the work, and he must be having trouble in finding a man or his ad would not be in today's paper. Try it. You can hint that you are prepared to turn a blind eye to Cookson's other activities. Eat humble pie if you like. Try him, anyway. Let me know how you get on and, of course, if you get the job . . . well, you know what I want. You have my phone number."

So I went. I had to admit to myself that the prospect of lucrative work, even for Cookson, took its share in persuading me. The Belsize Detective Agency charged twenty-five guineas a day, and an operative was paid ten pounds a day.

Cookson had a plush office off Regent Street.

He knew the value of appearances, and so did Gloria. It was she who engaged the office staff, and saw to it that the three girls employed were smart-looking, but not flashy, and dressed with decorum.

I had to wait in the small reception area off the landing on the first floor. Cookson was engaged with a client and the girl would not disturb him, or even send in my name, till the client had departed.

I had been there five minutes when Gloria came out to speak to the receptionist. She recognised me.

"Martin Yates, isn't it?" she asked. She was blonde now and getting plump. I had always classed her as a barmaid type, and now she looked more than ever like the girl who pulled me the odd pint in the local. Her greeting was cold, and there was a flicker of apprehension in her blue and somewhat prominent eyes. She knew all about me and the words I had exchanged with Cookson.

"Hallo, Gloria," I said easily. I had got to my feet, and that pleased her.

"You're looking prosperous," she ventured.

"I always look it. I never am. And you're . . ."

"Putting on weight," she laughed, slapping a tightly skirted hip. "Still, Cookie doesn't mind."

That was a laugh. He had weighed about seventeen stone himself the last time I had seen him.

She didn't ask me what I wanted, which was a relief, and when her business with the girl was finished went back into the office with a nod and a smile for me.

In ten minutes the client, a middle-aged woman and rather dowdy, scuttled out of the office as if she was ashamed of ever having been in it, and the girl phoned through my name.

"Go right in," she smiled surprisingly. "He says you know the way."

Cookson was in his office chair behind his expensive desk.

"Well, well, well!" he exclaimed, as if the sight of me was the biggest delight of the day, "Martin Yates. My dear old boy, I'm really glad to see you. Sit down."

His little dark eyes peeping out from the depths of his fat face were sparkling with bonhomie. I had seen them like black onyx with hate and venom. He was wearing a grey tweed suit of modest design, superbly cut. The Old

Boys' tie round his neck was as fraudulent as his cultured voice, but few would have questioned them. He had the fat man's genial personality, which he used to good effect.

"You're advertising a job, Cookie," I said, handing him the folded paper just as Everard had handed it to me. "I'd like it, if you'll be good enough to let bygones be bygones."

His eyes lost some of their twinkle, and he let the paper drop on to the desk without glancing at it.

"Fair do's, old boy," he protested. "I'd be a mug to re-employ you, wouldn't I?"

I had just sat down in the client's chair and now I got to my feet. It was on the tip of my tongue to tell him what I really thought of him, then I remembered Everard.

"I had second thoughts myself," I admitted. "It's asking a lot I know, but . . . well, I saw the ad last week and then when it came out again today I thought there might be a chance. I've had experience."

"Yeah." He waved a podgy hand. "Sit down, Martin. Big feller like you . . . makes me nervous to have you looming over me. As a matter of fact I put this ad in on behalf of a client. I sort the wheat from the chaff, so to speak, and then send the right types round to him. Come to think of it, you'd fit the bill, Martin. But the job's by way of being a menial one, if you know what I mean. You'd have to forget the ex-officer lark; that sort of thing."

"Well, what exactly is the job?" I asked impatiently, having already written it off as useless to Everard. "I'd make a lousy valet. Never could press my own pants, let alone anyone else's. Forget it, Cookie."

"No. No. You'd really fill the bill, Martin. My client's a millionaire. Bit of a crank, you'd call him, but when you've a bank balance the size of his you're entitled to a little eccentricity, eh? He insists on a man of strength and physical fitness, one who will give him unswerving loyalty, and one with no responsibilities or ties whatsoever. He's got a special project on hand, and he needs ... well ... a sort of body-guard."

"What's his name?" I asked idly, still not interested. Then I came back to earth, jarred right through to my spinal column.

"Reeves-Galway," Cookson said.

He may have seen my look of surprise, for he added quickly:

"Know him?"

"I've heard of him. I spend a good deal of time in the Scillies. I believe Reeves-Galway has built a house on St. Mary's. I'm sure I heard about it last time I was there. It's an unusual name . . ."

"You know the Scillies?" he cut in quickly. Now his eyes were hard with suspicion.

"Very well. Spent years there in my teens."

He picked up a Biro pen, and tapped the side of his fat face with it while he thought about things.

"No!" he declared harshly. "Scrub it, Martin. It's not the job for you. Sorry, and all that. I don't feel disposed to recommend you. And I've no job for you here. You know why. Nice to have seen you!"

I hesitated, astounded by his *volte-face* which had obviously been brought about by my mention of the Scillies.

"Beat it!" he snarled, stabbing the pen in the direction of the door.

I was tempted to lug him out of his chair by grabbing the lapels of his nice suit, telling him what I really thought, of him and then slapping him down hard in the hope of breaking the chair, as I had done the last time I had seen

24

him. Then Everard occurred to me. I simply turned on my heel and went out.

Three minutes later I had Everard on the phone from a public box in the Oxford Circus Underground.

"Suppose I try Reeves-Galway myself?" I suggested. "Seems to me there is something odd between Cookson and him. What the hell does he need a bodyguard for in the Scillies? It was mention of the Islands that frightened Cookson, I'm sure. Charles, can you get me Reeves-Galway's address? I daresay he's in London now if Cookson is recruiting for him. I'll be at the club within ten minutes."

"Suppose Cookson warns him about you?"

"Not a chance," I scoffed. "That fat villain holds me in as much contempt as I do him. I doubt if he'll trouble, because I was plainly not interested, and he was almost persuading me till I mentioned the Scillies."

"OK. I'll see what I can learn and ring you at the club."

I was having a cup of tea with Bill Stannard, who as it happened had put in a belated appearance, when Everard came through.

"Penthouse flat in Borleston House overlooking the park," he said. "He's at home at this moment. Have you thought how you are to explain your knowledge of the job that's going? You can't mention Cookson."

"I'll say that I heard he was recruiting staff when I was in Hugh Town, St. Mary's. He'll see nothing strange in that. Everybody knows everybody's business over there . . . amongst the residents, anyway."

"Wish you luck," Everard said. "Keep me informed."

It had stopped raining when I set out for Park Lane, and the June sunshine gleaming on the freshly washed streets and buildings was a tonic to my spirits.

Reeves-Galway's penthouse flat had its own lift. If I'd had any doubts about his status his London home would have dispelled them. You have to be stupidly rich to have a fountain, a pool, and supercilious goldfish in the pool, on the tenth-floor entrance to your pad. I had to get by an elderly butler who answered my ring. My guess was that he was a bigger snob than his master, so I used my rank on him, and that got me inside.

Reeves-Galway came out to greet me, and I realised that I had made a mistake with the butler, for it suggested that I was an equal, whereas I had come to get, if I could, a job below that of butler.

But I need not have worried. The mistake was Reeves-Galway's.

"I don't think I know you," he said stiffly, stopping short. "I was under the impression that I recognised your name. What do you want?"

He was a dark swarthy individual, powerfully built, with shoulders like those of a bull. He had blue eyes, but these appeared smeary, because the whites were in fact yellowish and bilious-looking. He was healthily tanned and he had an old-fashioned hair-line moustache. He reminded me of Douglas Fairbanks in an old television picture I had seen.

"I'm sorry to break in on you like this," I said, "but I heard while I was in the Scillies that you're looking for staff for your new house on St. Mary's. Can I offer my services? I need a job. I may not look it, but I'm broke. I can do the usual things: drive a car, sail a yacht, and even fly an aeroplane at a pinch, though the last would be a bit chancy."

His expression changed immediately, and he looked me up and down as if I was a hack he'd been offered cheap. I had asked for it in a way and I decided that it was the sort of treatment I must expect, though I was sure from that moment onwards that I was not going to like Mr. Reeves-Galway one bit.

"My butler said that you were a Captain Yates. What regiment?"

"Royal Marines."

"Commando?"

"Yes."

"That's good. You can take care of yourself, eh? As a matter of fact I'm advertising at the moment through an agent for a couple of likely men to act as bodyguards. I use the description for want of a better word, but it isn't strictly speaking that. I have a special project in hand in the Scillies and I want to avoid publicity of any sort. I loathe it. I would prefer a man who can devote his whole interest to me. I want a single man, with no dependants at all, who can go to the Scillies for three months, and keep his mouth shut. I don't want him to tell anybody that he's going. The Press will go to any lengths to get copy on me simply because I'm an extremely wealthy man. Stupid, but a fact. If they got even a hint that I'm taking on extra servants for the Scillies they'd be out there nosing around. Can you be relied upon to keep

28

your mouth shut? To tell no one where you are going? Not even a girl friend?"

"That's easy," I promised. "I never let girl friends know where I am as a matter of policy. I have only one relative: an old aunt who lives in Ireland."

He said nothing to that, but returned to looking me up and down. I expected him to ask me to turn round, or come and feel my biceps. It was an odd scrutiny, and it made me hot under the collar.

"Yes, it's my guess that you're superbly fit, Yates. I like that. I like strength in a man. I'm strong myself. I'd like to match mine against yours some day. Perhaps I will, if you get the job. I shall want references. The names of two men. Preferably two I can telephone. I don't want to be bothered writing letters."

"I can give you those now," I said taking out my notebook.

"Right. Let's have them."

He scribbled them down in his own notebook as I read them out.

"Good, and your phone number? I shall check on you and then ask you to call again for more details. I'm afraid that I shall not reveal my own name to your friends, but you'll understand that. The pay will be good Yates."

"I guessed that."

"I find that money buys most things. Even loyalty. I shall pay you a hundred pounds down in cash the day you're engaged and the balance also in cash at the end of the contract, another four hundred pounds."

I stared at him. Five hundred pounds for three months' menial work. Two thousand a year for a servant. He was a millionaire, but . . . What the hell was this project he had been talking about?

"Your phone number?" he asked.

I gave it to him and he wrote it down.

"Oh, Yates!" he called, as I was making for the door, "if you were in the Marines you must have known Colonel Sikes?"

It was a question and an important one to his mind. I could tell by the way he had put it. If I admitted that I had been well acquainted with Bill Sikes then I could kiss the job farewell. I knew it somehow. Perhaps it was instinct. Mention of the Scillies had scared Cookson, but not Reeves-Galway though I had taken care not to tell him that I was famlliar with the Islands.

But the elaborately casual way he had asked about Sikes was a warning.

"I've heard of him," I admitted. "I never served under him."

"But you must know that he met with a yachting accident in the Scillies?"

"I remember reading of it and hearing about it when I was in the Islands. To be honest, I didn't connect the name with a colonel in the Marines. Perhaps, I should have done. By all accounts he was first-class man. I'm sorry."

He nodded, and I went out. Two days later he rang me up asking me to call, and his butler, who by this time had learnt my true status in the establishment, escorted me into a study off the hall as if I was a bad smell he'd been unable to shake off.

Reeves-Galway was seated behind a plain desk not half as grand as Cookson's. He failed to greet me, or to ask me to sit down or even to tell me to stand at ease. He said:

"I've checked your references, Yates. You'll do. You can go over to the island and report to Coronel House as soon as you like. Here! Payment down."

He put a hand in the desk drawer and flung

me a packet of notes. Twenty fivers in a band. I caught them willingly.

"I shall be arriving by the ten o'clock helicopter on the first of July with my wife and small son. See you're at the airport with one of the cars; the eleven hundred for preference. It's the bigger of the two I keep there. Anything large like a Rolls is just an encumbrance on St. Mary's. You'll find a resident cook-housekeeper installed, and a sort of governess for the boy. He's at prep school now and if I take him away before term's end he has to be tutored at home. Building is somewhat restricted on the island and I was unable to put up as big a house as I would have liked. I even had a job to get permission for a double garage. So accommodation is limited and I'm not taking any staff from the mainland. You'll sleep over the garage with your opposite number a man named Chester, employed on the same terms as you. Any questions?"

"My duties?"

"I'll tell you the important one when I get there. In the meantime make yourself useful about the house and grounds. Plenty of work in the gardens. My yawl the *Dolphin* is in the harbour. You can keep her in trim; see the batteries are kept charged; that sort of thing. Damn it! If you leave today you'll be there barely a week before me. You don't want me to spell out what you need to do with yourself. And remember . . . no talk!"

I thanked him, and left. I had Everard on the phone within five minutes of leaving Borleston House, however, and wondered as I dialled the number what Reeves-Galway's reaction would have been had he known. I found his reason for secrecy, avoiding publicity, a little hard to swallow.

Everard was interested to hear of my success and we speculated on what Reeves-Galway's project might be but without reaching a solution. He asked me to call in the next morning at 10 a.m., and rang off.

I was in no hurry to get to the Scillies, and take up a role of odd-job man for a week. With Reeves-Galway's hundred pounds in my pocket perhaps I owed him the time, but he could afford it and I felt justified in spending some of it.

My visit to Everard resulted in my collecting a simple book code for communications. I could telephone him from St. Mary's but he didn't like the idea of phoning me at Reeves-Galway's house, and proposed to send me a coded telegram c/o The Post Office, Hugh Town. The wire would consist of a series of numerals which were page numbers, lines, and then the word counted from the margin. The book was an Everyman edition of *David Copperfield*.

I went away wishing that I had his faith in believing that Colonel Sikes had not met with a yachting accident but had been the victim of some mysterious plot involving Cookson and Reeves-Galway.

I left for Penzance by road on June 29th. My Mini-Cooper was practically in escrow to the garage people for non-payment of rent and I had to square the account before I could leave.

I reached the port at five o'clock and on my way into the town called in at the heliport on the off-chance of getting a flight that evening. But the chopper had been out of action all day with a damaged gearbox and there was a backlog of impatient holidaymakers waiting their turn. One harassed character in the crowd imparted information that BEA had only one machine on the Scillies run. The rest were on charter to the North Sea oil rigs. He sounded so indignant I said that he ought to sue them, and drove off to find a pub for the night.

The next morning I garaged the Mini at Taylor's close to the harbour and caught the *Scillonian*.

It was a fresh passage. Some of the unfortunates aboard would have called it more than that, but I enjoyed it. As far as I was concerned a sea breeze in my hair and the sun on my face, with the ship pitching into the Atlantic rollers, was long overdue. The sight of the Wolf Rock, lonely as hell as we passed to the north of it and the sea spuming white round its base, gave me a thrill, though I had viewed it countless times before.

The packet boats approach the harbour at Hugh Town either north of St. Mary's or south according to the state of the tide. On this occasion we went south through St. Mary's Sound close to Peninnis Head, with the cliffs rearing above us and dwarfing the ship.

As the *Scillonian* moved slowly towards the quay I could see that there had been a great deal of new building in Hugh Town since I had been there last, particularly on the Garrison overlooking the harbour, where the red flag with its white star of the Star Castle Hotel strained in the breeze. I wondered whereabouts exactly Coronel House was to be found on St.

Mary's sixteen hundred and ten acres, and what the costs had been. Though all the houses are built of the grey stone quarried on the island, everything else has to be ferried from the mainland and the price of a house is fantastic. This would not have worried Reeves-Galway, however.

There was the usual seething mob of disembarking passengers, those who had come to welcome them, idlers, boatmen and dogs milling around on the quay. I waited till it had thinned a little and the luggage had been hoisted ashore, then I picked out my two suitcases and sought the driver of one of Vic's minibus taxis.

The Scillonians, and the handful of taxi-drivers in particular, know every resident and house on their island. Vic's man grunted, "Oh aye," when I asked for Coronel House, as if he made the run three times a day.

He was in no hurry to move off. I sat in the bus smoking a cigarette enjoying the familiar scene. There was a magnificent white yacht moored out in the harbour. She was a yawl and I wondered if it was Reeves-Galway's. She was too far off the quay for me to read her name.

My eyes wandered ahead down the length of

the quay, and I received a minor shock. Two men and a girl were standing in a cluster at the quay's edge talking. Unless I was mistaken, and they were too far distant for me to be sure, one of the men was Cookson and the girl was his wife, Gloria.

I checked when the bus started and we passed the group slowly. It was Cookson all right, nattily dressed for holidaying, in knife-edged rust-coloured slacks, and a cream silk shirt fluttering in the breeze, with an Old Boy's striped cravat round his fat neck. Gloria was in pale blue stretch pants with a thin jersey, bulging with breastwork, to match. They were talking to a husky crew-cut character in khaki shorts and a red and white striped T-shirt. They looked at the bus as it passed, but I took care to turn towards a fellow passenger.

We made a miniature tour of Hugh Town, dropping off passengers here and there. The last couple were put down at Porth Mellon and then I was alone with the driver. He turned his bus to bring it back on to the island's main road, and we began climbing the hill past the road which I knew was the way to the airport, to turn left still climbing towards the Coastguard Station, a prominent landmark on the island.

"Where is the Coronel House then?" I asked the driver.

I think he was surprised to learn that I didn't know it.

"Along here, just short of the golf course. Fine house, only finished last month. Must have cost a mint. Belongs to a millionaire. They say he's arriving tomorrow. You a guest of his?"

"You could call me that," I agreed.

Presently he slowed the bus and turned into a semi-circular drive to put me down outside a long grey house; the tedium of its stone walls relieved by huge windows. It was all very new and spotless, with no sign that it had recently been in the hands of the builders. The gardens and lawns had already been lain and were flourishing. Between the house and the road was a wide stretch of recently mown grass striped immaculately by the passage of the mower. The edges of the drive and the concourse were lined with flower-beds filled with island flowers. I recognised the blue spiky blossoms of the agapanthus, that originated in South Africa and flourishes everywhere on the islands. The beautiful tongue-twister, the mesembryan-themum, was there in abundance, not only in

38

the beds but along the low wall dividing the property from the road.

While I was paying the driver, having unloaded my cases, a fawn-coloured eleven hundred swept into the drive and pulled up alongside.

The driver got out and strode over to me.

"You must be Yates," he said heartily, putting out a hand. "I'm Chester."

"I'm Yates," I agreed, shaking his hand, but not very enthusiastically. Chester was the crew-cut character I had seen talking so earnestly to Mr. and Mrs. Cookson down on the quay.

3

HIS sunburn made me look convalescent. He had pale blue eyes set somewhat close together in a long face, and he showed long yellowish teeth when he smiled. Given a pair of ears to match he would have looked like a horse, though in fact Chester's ears were small and close to his head.

He seemed friendly enough, though after seeing him on the quay with the Cooksons I couldn't trust him. Cookie had not wanted me on this job for some reason, and if Chester knew them it was a safe bet that Cookson had vetted him before sending him along to Reeves-Galway.

"The women are down the town shopping," Chester explained.

"Would that be the housekeeper?"

"Cook-housekeeper, Mrs. Peppiat and Meg Watkins the governess. Both locals. There's another girl Annie who does the general scivvying and comes in daily. She's practically a half-wit. Not easy to get labour on the island these days. I went down to meet you off the boat, but got waylaid by a couple of visitors I know."

"I saw you chatting. I was in the bus. Did you tell Cookie I was arriving today?"

He hadn't realised that I had seen them, and the news shook him.

"As a matter of fact I did. Why not?"

"How did you know I was arriving today?"

"Reeves-Galway phoned last night to ask if you'd got here. He said he'd told you to be here by the first . . . tomorrow. I worked out that you'd be on the boat. The chopper was out of action all day yesterday. What the hell is wrong about telling Cookson? He interviewed me and sent me along to the boss. Didn't he do the same for you?"

"Not quite. He turned me down and I went along to Reeves-Galway myself. How did Cookie take the news?"

Chester got a grip on one of my cases.

"I'll show you where we bunk," he said. "Over the garage. Not bad at all."

"You haven't answered my question," I said.

"He didn't like it, if you must know," he replied leading the way along the front of the house to the garage.

There were stairs at the back and we went up these to enter a small flat. Chester had installed himself in the front room, probably because the other had been designed as a lounge and a door to the kitchen and bathroom led out of it. But the room had been furnished as a bed-sitter regardless of expense, and I had no kick. There was a divan bed, a tall compactum, a solid armchair in hide, and a small desk with chair to match. The carpet of blue nylon was flush-fitted. The view from the wide window was magnificent. I put down my case and went to lean upon the sill.

The land sloped gently downwards from the back of the house where there was nearly an acre of lawn and gardens vivid with flowers. The bottom of the lawn, which showed only faint traces that it had recently been laid from turves, cradled a swimming pool in which the water was bluer than the sea a few hundred yards distant. Away to the right I could see the fairways of the golf course and the tall metal masts of the radio beacons. Beyond the golf course over a strip of sparkling sea I could take my fill of Trescoe, its long silver beach clearly visible backed by the woods surrounding the Abbey. Left of it were the twin peaks of

Samson, and a glim
left my gaze went ⋯
eight miles distant, ar
more to the south se⋯
Town and the harbour
to the quay on a dropp

It was familiar and y
lovely under the brill
suddenly I was glad to ⋯ any
condition.

"Like it?" Chester asked at my elbow. "Boy, I'm telling you this is a swell place. The air is about the clearest I've ever known. You'll need to watch the sunbathing. Go easy on it for a day or so. Never known it burn so much, not even in the south of Spain. Kind of peaceful too. No cars to speak of and the folks are real friendly."

"Yet Reeves-Galway needs a couple of body-guards," I pointed out.

"Yeah," he agreed. "Kind of screwy if you ask me. But I'm not grumbling. The pay is fantastic, the bed is soft, and Ma Peppiat's cooking is out of this world."

Chester plumped his bulk on to the bed.

"What goes between you and Cookson, then? He told me not to let on to you that he was on

...e seen him sooner or later,
...and is a mighty small place."

...to know that Cookson is a crook,"
...h. "Whether or not Reeves-Galway
...it is anyone's guess. Have you any idea
...at this special duty is that he has in mind for
us?"

"Nope. All he told me was that he loathes
publicity, and asked me not to let on that I was
taking a job with him in the Scillies." Chester
scratched his bristly head. "For his sort of
money I'm the original oyster, but there's no
reason why you and I shouldn't discuss it. If
this Cookson is bent, how would a rich guy like
Reeves-Galway come to use him?"

It was becoming obvious to me that Chester
was genuine. He had seen the advertisement,
answered it and been given the job. He knew
nothing more.

"Cookie is a smart number," I said. "I don't
suppose Reeves-Galway knows any more about
him other than his being a private eye who
could reasonably be expected to produce a
couple of bodyguards."

I started unpacking, stowing my things into
the compactum, which had far more clothes
hangers than I possessed suits.

Chester told me about himself. He'd had three years in the Army, a spell in the Metropolitan Police as a squad-car driver, a milk roundsman's job that had lasted six weeks, and then he had gone to Australia, where he'd been a lifeguard. He had been out there for three years before he had wanted to see home again, but he'd had to work his passage back and that had taken him round the world. He had crewed on a yacht for two summers, spending the winters in a Blackpool bingo hall, and needing a change had cast around all spring without any luck till he had answered Cookson's ad.

Chester was perfectly frank, and I hadn't a doubt that he had told me the truth. His background was a very ordinary one. He had been a bombardier in the Army, and a constable in the police force. Without feeling in any way superior to him I had to admit that he and I had nothing in common, except possibly our build. I pointed this out to him, without I was sure in any way offending him.

"OK," he grinned, "if we make a team you can be the brains. I never had any to speak of."

"I wasn't thinking of that exactly. I was wondering if there is a common denominator

45

that has not been mentioned. What sort of questions did Cookson ask you before he sent you along to Reeves-Galway?"

"Personal ones, mostly. Was I married? Did I have any dependents? Girl friends? Brothers or sisters?"

"And have you?" I asked quickly.

"Nary a one. I went straight out of an orphanage into the Boy's Battery in the Gunners. I don't even know how I came by name."

"And I have no relatives save one ancient aunt in Ireland. We have that much in common."

"What are you getting at?" he wanted to know.

"I'm not sure."

I was still nervous of letting him know my real reason for being in the Scillies. It may have been instinct, on the other hand, telling me that Stephen Chester, which was the full name he knew nothing of, was dead straight, and I needed an ally. I decided to give him the full story. I put him in the picture while I finished unpacking.

"Cripes!" he declared with feeling when I had related everything, "I don't like the sound of it. But supposing the big-shot meets Cookson when he arrives? Ain't he going to give you the sack?"

"Perhaps. It depends on how badly he needs us on this special project. If he does then I go, but I won't leave the island. I'll be around and you can keep me in the picture. Always provided you're willing, and don't mention a word of this to Reeves-Galway?"

He got up from the bed and strolled over to the window.

"I was going to enjoy this job," he declared, waving a hand at the view. "One of the prettiest spots in the world. Now you've made me nervous. You know something? I knew Blagdon. He and I were in the same division for a while. Everyone from the station sergeant to the superintendent knew he was taking graft. They got him in the end, of course, and slung him out."

"Can you describe him?"

"Yeah. He was a big ginger-haired bastard, ugly as sin. I'm no oil painting, but he *looked* mean. I can't remember any individual feature. Too long ago. Why d'you ask?"

"Because if the body was his the trail stopped at Penzance, but he could have come to the Islands using another name. I might be able to find somebody who remembers him. Sikes, Reeves-Galway and Cookson were all here last year."

Chester gazed moodily at the view, his hands in the pockets of his shorts. I made a quick change into flannels and a sports shirt. He was obviously brooding over what I had told him, and it was not until I was buttoning my shirt after a quick visit to the bathroom for a wash-up that he had any more to say.

"Yep!" he announced suddenly. "I'm inclined to agree with your pal Everard about what happened, or rather didn't happen, to Sikes. I crewed on a private yacht for two seasons. I know what I'm talking about. He wouldn't have gone overboard in a moderate sea. If he did, then someone helped him over. His body should have turned up by now after nearly three months. This ain't the middle of the Pacific. Plenty of beaches for it to fetch up on, and no big fish to eat it.

"Blagdon's was weighted by the feet but turned up within that time," I agreed. "That's what makes me think he was dumped off the Scillies. The tides round here are fierce enough to have ripped him off any anchor. He ought to have had a concrete overcoat."

At that moment we heard the sound of a car on the drive, and then it came into the garage beneath us.

"That'll be the women back," Chester said. "I'll go down and tell 'em you're here. Lunch will be any minute now. See you."

He grinned and went out. I heard him leaping down the stairs.

I gave them a few minutes to get over the shock, and then went down to walk along a flagged terrace behind the house.

Chester came out of the kitchen door as I approached.

"Come on in," he invited.

I hadn't given much thought to the feminine menials in the household whose company I would have to enjoy, if I could, for three months. Meg Watkins, having been given the label of tutor or governess, I had dismissed as being something dowdy. Annie had been described as a half-wit and Mrs. Peppiat could only offer me the quality of her cooking.

I went in and Chester introduced me casually enough to all three at the same time. Annie, who was a straight-haired wench and mouselike, was working at the sink. She giggled. Mrs. Peppiat was a stout white-haired body with a bright red face, who nodded genially. Miss Watkins I stared at quite unashamedly.

She was laying the big kitchen table for the coming meal, and, far from being dowdy, she was a stunner. She was wearing the briefest of pale green shorts with a shirt to match. Her long legs were beautifully tanned. She had short butter-coloured hair, elegantly tousled, a sweet face helped by a generous mouth, and big grey eyes. She too nodded her greeting.

Mrs. Peppiat asked me if I'd had a good crossing, to which I replied: "Yes thank you," and returned my gaze to the delectable Miss Watkins.

She continued laying the table, placing the knives and forks with neat precision, then paused before she reached for the dessert spoons.

"Do you usually stare at people, Mr. Yates?" she enquired. "It's very rude."

"That depends on the people," I smiled. It didn't thaw her at all and she went on laying the dessert forks and spoons. The air seemed a little frigid. Chester, leaning against the dresser and pulling at the lobe of his right ear, remarked that the lunch smelt good. Mrs. Peppiat volunteered the information that it was a beef casserole. Presently Miss Watkins finished at the table and said:

"Steve tells me that you used to be a frequent visitor to St. Mary's, Mr. Yates?"

"That's right. Had an uncle who owned a farm above Pelistry Bay."

I saw that her grey eyes were laughing.

"Mr. Barrow," she supplied. "I remember playing in the summer holidays with a schoolboy from the mainland. His name was Martin Yates. He was a horrible big boy always frightening me with a flick knife. I hope you've improved since those days!"

I cast my mind back over the years. There had always been a little gang of us made up of visitors and neighbouring Islanders. Two or three girls. What the hell had been their names? Yes, there had been a Maggie Watkins, a tall scrawny wench with steel-rimmed glasses always slipping down her nose.

"Good Grief!" I exploded. "Maggie!"

"Meg now," she said firmly, "and don't you forget it."

Over lunch I learnt more about her. She told me that along with the brighter kids from the Islands she had gone as a boarder to the mainland at school in Redruth, and from there on a

51

scholarship to Lady Margaret Hall at Oxford. She was hoping for a post in Hugh Town's new school where the island children would now be getting secondary education up to A levels. Her father and mother were still living at Pelistry Bay and she had wanted her attendance at Reeves-Galway's house to be on a daily basis, but he had insisted on her living in. For a month she was to be a tutor to Master Felix Reeves-Galway, and thereafter act as a sort of governess till the end of September. The pay, of course, was exceptional and she had not argued about living in Coronel House.

On the boss's orders she had written to the boy's so-called prep school, virtually little more than a nursery school, and learnt that Felix's accomplishments were practically nil. At the age of seven the child could hardly read or add up. Hers seemed a gargantuan task for Reeves-Galway had struck me as being the sort who would expect more in a month from a tutor than a whole year at school.

"The kid may lead you a hell of a dance if you're not careful," I warned her.

"I can cope," she answered confidently.

After lunch our time was our own till the Reeves-Galways arrived next morning. Chester said that he would mow the lower lawn after which he would get himself some more tan by the swimming pool. Meg was going home for the rest of the day using the Mini.

I hung around with Chester till mid-afternoon, then taking the eleven hundred buzzed down to Hugh Town, and the public telephone box outside the Post Office. I got through to Everard with hardly any more delay than if I had been calling him from the club, and reported my arrival. He was interested to learn that Cookson was on the island, and promised me a full description of Blagdon.

I backed out of the box, and a well-remembered voice said: "Hallo, Martin."

I turned to see Cookson's elegant if corpulent figure standing on the narrow pavement. My reaction was to wonder if he could possibly have overheard my conversation with Everard, but I decided against it. He would have needed to have brought his bulk close to the glass panels of the box, and I would have known he was there by his shadow.

His greeting had not exactly been cordial and his little black eyes were snapping with hate.

"I want a word with you," he piped. His voice always went shrill when he was roused.

"I'm not so sure that I want one with you," I retorted, "but fire away."

"Not here," he said. "Too public."

I led the way into the alley beside the Post Office, which I knew would take us on to a narrow road that joined another which would bring us to the foot of Garrison. However, it went steeply uphill and hauling his fat up a gradient was not Cookie's idea of a pleasant afternoon.

"This will do," he gasped before we had joined the garrison road. "It's quiet enough here."

So it was. With the afternoon's launches gone with the bulk of the visitors Hugh Town's back streets dozed in the sun.

"So you pulled a fast one on me," he panted. "You went round to Reeves-Galway, and got him to take you on himself."

"And you've lost your commission, Cookie. I am sorry," I said gravely.

"Commission my backside!" he rasped crudely. "It doesn't suit me to have you on the job. Maybe I can get him to sack you but your peculiar physical attributes, your Commando training . . ."

"What the hell do you mean by my peculiar

physical attributes?" I demanded. "Are you suggesting the man is a queer?"

"He's queer all right, old boy, but not in the way you think. But skip that. I don't know what he's paid you in advance but I'll double it if you'll jack it in and leave the island."

I shook my head.

"Nothing doing," and when he showed signs of increasing the offer, added, "Save your breath, Cookie. You'll need it hauling that fat carcass around."

"Okay!" he snapped, his face crimson, "if that's the way you want it. Remember, I warned you. I can get you taken care of, even here. If you've got any sense, Yates, and God knows you must have some, you'll get on the four o'clock boat." He glanced at his watch. "That gives you thirty-five minutes!"

4

HE stared at me malevolently over the arm he had raised to bring up his watch, then he lunged off down the hill, fury in every lumbering stride.

"You're joking!" I called after him, but he took no notice.

I gave him a minute or two to get out of sight then went back to the spot where I had parked the eleven hundred.

That evening after dinner, Chester, who had been on the island for nearly two weeks, revealed the fact that he had found himself a girl friend in the town. She worked in the Atlantic Hotel and her evening duties finished at nine. On the strong supposition that Reeves-Galway would not take kindly to him dashing off to meet girls on the island he wanted to see her again while he had the chance. He was apologetic about it, because he thought I expected him to keep me company. I didn't, but I kept it to myself, for I was finding Chester, after you had got over his somewhat sinister appearance induced by his closely set eyes and cropped head, a likable character engagingly frank and above board.

Ma Peppiat had her own armchair in the kitchen which was set about four feet from the television screen. This was her sole relaxation. Annie, who was a daily, had wobbled off homewards on an ancient bike shortly before dinner. I kept wishing Meg Watkins was there. I had thought about her a lot, and her startling transformation from the scrawny kid I had known twelve years ago.

"Would you like to look over the yawl?" Chester offered. "I'm going down town in the eleven hundred. The dinghy's beached behind Holgate's. Only snag is you may have to walk back." He grinned.

"Will have to you mean," I corrected him. "I don't mind that."

"OK. I'll get the keys. You might check over her batteries. You'll find a hydrometer in the engine cubby."

He parked the car outside Holgate's, which is a forty-bedroomed hotel, the owner of which has gone into retirement and no longer takes in guests, then led me down the side of the hotel to the beach and the dinghy. He helped me lug it down to the water.

Reeves-Galway's yawl was the big white one I had seen from the quay while waiting in the taxi. Her name was the *Dolphin*. Not very original, perhaps, but apt for a creature of the sea.

The dinghy's Evinrude fired after a couple of pulls. I waved to Chester, and was soon buzzing over the smooth water of the harbour towards the yawl.

No man can spend all the summer months of his life up till his late teens in the Scillies, and then eight years of service life mostly afloat as I had done, without getting a love for ships. The *Dolphin* was a beautiful craft. She was white overall. She had no bowsprit but the railing at her pulpit was flared and shaped so that her lines were perfect.

I secured the dinghy, got the covers off her and went aboard. Her decking was a lovely teak. The sailing gear was the last word in mechanical handling and the masts were metal. I guessed her displacement at twenty tons, and she must have cost Reeves-Galway close on thirty thousand pounds. The man's money choked me. The thought that he used her for little more than pottering round the Islands like some form of marine bus twisted my guts.

I explored the ship from stem to stern. She was lavishly appointed and you could have sailed her round the world. She was fitted with a Perkins diesel. All the controls were to hand on a dash fitted in front of the helmsman's chair in the cockpit. Under power she could be sailed single-handed.

For a while I stood by the helm and let my imagination go wild. She belonged in the open sea. In my mind's eye I could see her heaving to the swell; see the water coming green over her dipping bows and hear the wind thrumming past her stays. When I put a hand on the wheel I could imagine its feel as I held her on course. She was the most beautiful creation of man I had ever set eyes upon, and I wished she was mine. Envy is nothing but stupidity and I avoid it if I can, but at that moment I envied Reeves-Galway so much it was like a physical pain.

I discovered that there was an auxiliary motor for charging her batteries when I had the hatches off her tiny engine room. I tested the batteries. They were down a bit. I decided that I could spare a couple of hours aboard, so I got the generator going. There was nothing to running it, since there was an automatic governor, but the two-stroke motor made a racket till I had the hatches on again.

I found that the time passed quickly pottering round the ship. I explored every locker, cupboard and cabin aboard. Maybe I ought not to have done, but the cleverness of her design and the resulting storage space fascinated me. I made one odd discovery that puzzled me. In the owner's cabin, which was cunningly appointed, with cupboards built into the bulkhead, my eye was caught by a long flat and leather-covered case lying along a shelf. Though the ship had been well stocked with stores, spares, charts, and a veritable Fortnum and Mason's of tinned foods in her pantry, there were no personal belongings aboard. This must have made me curious about the case. I took it down fingering its red leather cover. It was not locked and when I hinged up the lid it was to see two knives set in velveted recesses. Each had about six inches of wickedly sharp double-edged blade and four inches of handle; rosewood, I thought.

I picked one out and hefted it in my hand. It was beautifully balanced, and knowing something of knives I was tempted to throw it, but there was no target handy and Reeves-Galway wouldn't have thanked me for spoiling his sycamore-panelled bulkhead. Instead I switched on the cabin light for dusk was settling rapidly outside, and examined the knife closely, wondering if this one or its mate had ever been used.

I decided, when I had taken out the other and examined it against its fellow, that the first one had a stain high up on the blade and that close to the guard under the handle there was a trace of dried blood.

I put them back into the case and replaced it on the cupboard shelf. There was a small bar in the saloon, well stocked with a catholic array of new bottles, and I helped myself to a whisky on the assumption that my labours to date deserved it.

I took it out to the cockpit. The tide was ebbing, and the *Dolphin* moored at her bows had swung stern to the west where the sun was setting like a gigantic red ball between the twin peaks of Samson. The whole of the western sky was flooded with every shade of flaming orange and red. Sunsets in the Scillies are really something, and this one was awe-inspiring in its extent and colour.

I wondered what the hell Reeves-Galway

needed with a couple of throwing knives. Protection of a sort? If he had planned at one time to sail to far away places; to scummy ports in the tropics, he might have thought it necessary to carry armament aboard. A rifle, or an automatic, and maybe a couple of knives. The guns, of course, would have had to be turned in on a return to the UK unless a licence had been obtained, which might not have been granted.

It was none of my business, though the fact that one showed traces of blood made it difficult to forget until I reminded myself that it was not necessarily human blood.

I stayed aboard till it was properly dark. There was no moon, but the stars were brilliant, and their reflections shimmered on the water shifting restlessly on the tiny waves in the harbour. I shut down the generator, and in the resulting silence the sound of music came along a carpet of red neon light, both from the restaurant on the quay.

The covers were wet with dew when I locked up and dropped into the dinghy. I unhitched it, and concentrated on finding the toggle handle of the starting cord in the dark.

I'd not given a thought to Cookson, and what

I considered his idle threat, since I had seen him that afternoon. Maybe I should have done, but it is difficult to reconcile the happy sun-drenched life of the Scillies with murder and sudden death.

There were two of them in a dinghy, and they had been waiting motionless, except for an odd paddle or two to combat the tide, a few yards off the *Dolphin*'s quarter ready to glide in as soon as I was in the dinghy. They had probably planned a drowning.

But in the dark they mucked it. The man at the oars pulled too sharply with his right hand so that instead of coming alongside they came in at an angle and their prow struck mine, warning me of their presence before the man who was to board me was ready. I had a moment in which to see his dark amorphous shape, seemingly as big as a house, coming down on me as I knelt at the stern. Countless lessons from tough Marine instructors made my reactions instant and automatic. I backhanded him with the cutting edge of my palm, hoping for his neck but in fact by the feel of it catching him across the side of his face. He must have seen too many lights to know any more till he hit the water over the stern after I had caught a leg and pitched him with reasonable accuracy.

The dinghy was well-nigh capsized by the violence, and I found myself sitting on its floor boards. I think the thrusting efforts of the man who had come aboard had pushed the other dinghy clear. At any rate when I gave it my attention it was too far for me to reach, and its occupant was tugging furiously at an oar in order not to bring it back but to go after his pal who had come to the surface, making watery shouts.

Both dinghies had gone on the tide clear of the *Dolphin* and so had the man in the water. His pal was skilful enough in reaching him with the dinghy but he couldn't get him aboard.

"Give me a hand!" he yelled. "He's like a bloody log, and can't swim!"

"Go to hell!" I yelled back.

I didn't believe it for a moment. No man would have attempted to attack me in a dinghy, doubtless with the idea of bustling me overboard, unless he could swim, and swim well, himself. The fellow in the dinghy probably thought I was mug enough to paddle over to him so that he could have another go.

I found the starting cord at last and the Evinrude roared into life. I made the beach without incident, and lugged her clear of the high-tide level, marked by a line of weed. Then I waited gently rubbing the heel of my right hand.

Presently it occurred to me that they might make for the quay on their return, and although there were lights along it I was too far away to distinguish figures, so I moved along the sand until I reckoned I would be able to see them as they walked along it after tying their dinghy. If they beached up by Holgate's where I had done then I would see them on the water before they arrived. But they never came, and after a long wait I considered it safe to assume that they had come off another yacht. I'd make it my business to discover which, but not that night.

I walked back to Coronel House, and I walked warily in case I had missed them coming ashore. But nothing happened. Chester was still out and I heard the car return and drive into the garage at about one in the morning. He crept upstairs fearful of waking me. I decided against telling him anything, turned over and went to sleep.

I was up at the airport in good time to meet the Reeves-Galways, standing beside the parked eleven hundred, and feeling like a dowager's chauffeur.

The chopper was five minutes late. I saw it first overland. It came round low in a big circle, hovered and settled down. The long fuselage slung below its huge rotors made it look like a giant bird of prey coming in with its kill in its claws.

The proceedings for its arrival were informal. The exact spot on to which it was settling appeared to have been decided by the parking of Vic's airport bus on the grass opposite the fire station, nowhere near the tarmac square and the control tower farther up the road.

The helicopter touched down, sunk on its wheels, rose again, the pilot cut his motor, the rotors died, drooped, and the visitors began filing out of the machine's belly on to the grass for the short walk to the bus.

Reeves-Galway and family were next but last to leave the helicopter. Having met him I was now more interested in seeing his wife. Chester, who was well briefed on film stars, had told me that her name was Lola. I would probably have spotted her even if she had not been accompanied by Reeves-Galway, for she was in a gold trouser suit, with her thick dark hair

66

bound into a bouncing top-knot by a gold bandeau. She was an eyeful. Her voluptuous figure, even in trousers, and her slinky walk were a greater attraction to some of the visitors than the immediate beauties of the island.

Reeves-Galway kept a pace ahead of her, and Master Felix trailed in the rear, turning and shuffling backwards, unable to take his eyes off the helicopter.

When they came up to the car Reeves-Galway said to her: "This is Yates," as if I was part of the scenery.

But for their eyes you could have thought he was Italian, for he was swarthy enough, and she English by her complexion, which appeared flawless. Her eyes were like dark velvet, big and exciting, with a faintly impudent look. The sex oozed from her.

"How do you do, Yeets?" she said in a quaint and husky accent.

"His name is Yates," Reeves-Galway growled, and then to me "Fetch the luggage, will you? There are two cases on the plane. The remainder is on the *Scillonian*. Make a note to get it up to the house as soon as the ship arrives this morning. Get in, Felix," he barked at the boy impatiently.

I sensed that the kid was not altogether happy. Reeves-Galway, I thought, was not the type to be a successful father. He would expect constant and immediate obedience without offering any sort of affection in return. In spite of his money his adopted son appeared a scruffy little number. He was a weed of a child, with a thin nervous face under a shock of unruly fair hair, and legs like matchsticks. He obviously lacked a mother's close attention. His red blazer was faded with age and had been well spotted by his last ice-cream. His school tie had been reduced to a distorted and knotted rag. One of his stockings was wrinkled halfway down a leg. I wondered if Meg was expected to straighten him out. It was obvious that Lola gave him about as much attention as she would a cheese mite from one of her native gorgonzolas.

I went over to the helicopter where the luggage was already being brought out of the hold beneath the pilot's cabin. After careful searching I rescued the two cases from being slung into Vic's bus and carried them to the car. They were moderately sized and I was able to get them in the Morris's small boot.

Reeves-Galway had already taken the wheel

with the boy beside him, which meant that I had to squeeze into the back with Lola.

"Come in, Yeets," she smiled, as if she was inviting me into her boudoir.

I piled in.

Reeves-Galway drove as if he was on the last leg of the Monte Carlo Rally and running late. The tyres screamed as we curved round the bottom of the airfield. The motion threw his wife against me and I was enveloped in a cloud of Chanel.

"I hang on, yes?" she whispered, her dark eyes flinging out the age-old challenge. She had some excuse, but she continued to press against me, holding me by an arm. Her leg against mine was firm and warm and infinitely exciting.

I thought: Watch it, Yates. You won't last under this sort of treatment. La Lola was definitely disturbing.

Then the boy opened the window on his side. Clear of the airfield we were dropping down the hill to the T-junction at the bottom. The speed at which we were travelling, allied to a fresh westerly blowing, let in a gale and Lola forgot me to scream at him to shut the window.

The kid piped: "Shan't!"

His father bawled: "Do as you're told!"

The boy took no notice and Reeves-Galway leant across him with his left hand to wind up the offending window, without, however, slackening speed. I shut my eyes. We took the right angle turn somehow and tore up the slight hill to the next T-junction. We made the left turn, but it flung the girl my way again. She hung on for fifty yards and then Master Felix obligingly opened the window once more.

Lola's reaction was to lean over and cuff him, screeching a few Italian epithets at him. Reeves-Galway did his one-hand window-winding act by stretching across the two of them, regardless of the fact that we were fast approaching the junction of the island's main road.

They were still cursing the kid when we arrived at the house after a total journey of not more than a mile.

The staff had turned out to greet their lord and master. Mrs. Peppiat bobbed. Annie giggled. Chester saluted. Meg smiled, and grabbed hold of the boy.

"So you're Felix! Heavens, what a mess! This way, Felix."

She led him into the house by an ear. The kid was speechless through sheer stupefaction at such commanding treatment.

I happened to glance at Lola, who had been watching Meg.

Miss Watkins had dressed for duty in a brief grey skirt and white blouse. Their stark simplicity emphasised the natural perfection of her features and the superb lines of her figure. She looked as fresh and as clean as a flower picked from the garden on a dewy morn, and made the Italian girl seem something exotic and forced from the hot house. Lola's lips were compressed and her eyes glinting. She didn't like competition.

"Yates! Chester!" Reeves-Galway barked, "I want words with you."

We followed him into the house, and he led the way into what was known as the study. It was a room on a corner, with small windows on two sides, and beautifully furnished like the rest of the place. Mrs. P had decorated it with vases of flowers cut from the garden. I daresay the floral touch had been charming with the room empty, but somehow with Reeves-Galway there the flowers struck a jarring note.

He slumped into a padded chair behind the flat-topped desk. He failed to ask us to sit down, and we stood in front of him rather like prisoner and escort up before the CO.

"I think the time has come," he began without further preamble, "to tell you why I have hired you at, I would point out, very handsome wages. I don't really need bodyguards, though later you may have to adopt those roles." He looked at me. "I asked you if you had heard of Colonel Sikes, you remember? He has now been missing close on three months. I think he was murdered and his body buried on one of the uninhabited islands. We are going to search for his grave, quietly and methodically, at night."

I glanced at Chester, whose mouth had come open in astonishment, revealing his long horse-like teeth.

"What makes you so certain Sikes was murdered?" I asked the boss, who had opened a drawer in the desk and taken out a box of Perfectos.

"If he had gone overboard and been drowned it is a certainty that his body would have been found by now."

He held the cigarette in his fingers. Perhaps he was used to a flunkey rushing forward with a light, but neither Chester nor I obliged.

"Are you crazy?" I demanded.

It was a most unfortunate question, intended

72

to be purely rhetorical, and not to be expected from a menial. The effect on Reeves-Galway was astonishing, as if for a moment he was going into a fit. His eyes bulged and his fingers shook, crumbling the cigarette. He recovered himself.

"By God, Yates," he mouthed, "if you ever speak to me like that again I'll not only fire you I'll knock the living daylights out of you as well!"

It was the sort of talk that normally would have brought a short answer and rapid action from me. I think Chester realised it, because he put a warning hand on my arm. However, I kept a grip on myself. If you must accept odd jobs for exorbitant pay, I told myself, then you must expect odd treatment from odd characters. Aloud, I said:

"I beg your pardon. The question was not meant literally. To search the uninhabited islands for a grave is a hell of a task. You must be very sure that Sikes was murdered. Why? Do you mean he was boarded and killed. What for? He wouldn't have been carrying much money. Thirty or forty pounds in his wallet. Maybe less. It doesn't add up."

He found another cigarette and a light for it.

He drew on it and the smoke curled out of his nostrils. He looked suddenly cunning and furtive. I couldn't make the man out.

"I happen to know," he said, "that Sikes was a smuggler. He smuggled diamonds. They were doubtless the target the night he was killed."

5

CHESTER and I digested the implications behind Reeves-Galway's remark in silence. It was on the tip of my tongue to ask him how he knew Sikes had been a smuggler, but I thought better of it. He would resent the question, and I had already upset him. I realised that I knew next to nothing of Sikes, though I would not have excepted the role of a diamond-smuggler from a man in his position. Everard had described him as being moderately wealthy, which suggested that he would have had no need to engage in such a dangerous racket for profit. All the same, he might have been doing it for kicks, and if he had, and had been carrying stones on his yacht, then his murder was a distinct possibility.

Chester cleared his throat.

"We'll need plenty of the right equipment, sir," he said.

Reeves-Galway sat back in his chair and showed white teeth in a smile. "Thank you, Chester," he beamed. "At least you are prepared to go along with the idea. And you, Yates?"

"Of course if Sikes was a smuggler then it throws an entirely different light on his disappearance. May I ask if you have informed the police?"

"Of my suspicions? Yes. I have no proof to offer them. I think that they believe him to have been dumped overboard in deep water."

"Isn't that the mostly likely supposition?" I asked.

Reeves-Galway moved his massive shoulders in the semblance of a shrug.

"Perhaps. I happen to think otherwise. I'm sure that if he had been put overboard his body would have been found by now. Tides are strong in these waters, and even if the body had been weighted . . ." He paused. "Decomposition would break it up, free parts of it from the weight." He shook his head. "Some part of it would have been found by now."

I remember that in London I had pretended ignorance of Sikes and his disappearance other than what I had read in the papers. I thought it would be better to keep it that way. Chester seemed prepared to stand and await orders.

76

"Why are you so keen to find Sikes' body, sir?" was my next question.

"Because he was a friend of mine, Yates, and I don't like the idea of his murderers getting away with it. Besides, it gives me an objective."

"Finding his body is not necessarily going to find his murderers," I pointed out.

"Ah!" he beamed, "now you've put your finger right on it. I think that they are still in the neighbourhood. I also think that word of what we are doing will get about. It will be a dicey situation, for publicity is the last thing I want, but if they suspect what we are up to, looking for a grave, then I think they might make efforts to stop us, and that is why I have hired you two chaps. They might, for instance, threaten me through my family. Then indeed I shall need you in the roles of bodyguards."

"Have you any idea of who they are?" I asked, recalling the two gentleman in the dinghy and their abortive attempt to put me in the harbour. "I mean, do you think that they are operating from a ship?"

"More than likely, Yates. I don't know how Sikes worked his smuggling racket. I can guess. Ships coming in from the Atlantic pass within a few miles of the Bishop, some even closer. It would be simple for one of the crew to drop a floating canister overboard for a lone yachtsman to pick up by the light of a full moon, having received word by radio. Don't you agree?"

It was feasible. Knowing the seas usually prevailing round the Bishop, the canister would need to be well marked. In these days of ultra-short-wave-radio, communication would be the least of the difficulties. A transmitter, battery-powered and with a range of twenty miles, could go in a seaman's kit and take no more room than a paperback. Yes, it could have been done. Sikes had possibly been hi-jacked, and his haul stolen. But I found it hard to believe that they had taken the trouble to land his body on one of the uninhabited islands and bury it. The whole thing would have been planned, and, tides or no tides, they would have known enough about keeping a body down in deep water to dump him overboard. So much more convenient.

"When do you propose to start?" I asked.

"Tonight. Why not? The necessary gear is aboard the *Scillonian* with the remainder of the luggage. When you go down to collect it I want you to transfer a large crate—it contains shovels, pickaxes, lamps, everything we need—

to the *Dolphin*. You've been looking after the yawl, I hope?"

"She's in good trim, sir," Chester said.

Reeves-Galway said, "Right!" and we dismissed.

The *Scillonian* announced her arrival outside the harbour by a blast on her siren. As soon as we heard it, approaching midday, Chester and I took off in the eleven hundred and were down on the quay waiting before she had tied up.

"Why are we hurrying?" he wanted to know. "It'll be twenty minutes before they're ready to unload the baggage."

I parked the car behind the Customs and we strolled to the quay's edge. I told him what had happened the previous night when I had been about to leave the *Dolphin*.

He whistled.

"They don't waste time," he agreed.

"I'm pretty sure they came from another yacht, and I'd like to know which one. If we can identify her then we can make a few enquiries, such as . . . was she here last April when Sikes disappeared?"

Chester pulled thoughtfully at his right ear. It was very pleasant down on the quay under the brilliant noonday sun. The usual crowd had gathered to welcome the steamer. Launches that would take passengers to the off-shore islands were fussing alongside the quay, and manoeuvring about the harbour.

"I get you," Chester said. "You think that Cookson could be tied in with the hi-jackers. Is that it?"

"I wouldn't be surprised to learn that he organised it. I wouldn't put murder past that fat so-and-so. He was here last year. He was here in April, ostensibly on holiday. He's here now. He may be fat, but he's not the type to waste time lounging in the Scillies. I think he was here on business."

"Yeah, but what knocks me is that a wealthy guy like Reeves-Galway employs him . . ."

"Cookie can play the gentleman when he wants. He probably scraped acquaintance with him when they were staying in Delgardens in April. The point is—has Cookson got round to considering why Reeves-Galway needs us in the Scillies? Has he guessed that the big-shot is going searching for a grave? If he has, Steve, then we're in for trouble."

I let my eyes rove over the yachts moored in the harbour. There were several small cutters, three of them flying the French flag. There were two ketches, and a big old motor-cruiser, dirty as a tramp. The *Dolphin* was undoubtedly queen of them all.

"Any ideas?" I asked Chester.

"I reckon they'd need a power boat and a good sea boat at that if they were using her for hi-jacking a yacht. Something like that old scow over there."

He nodded towards the motor-cruiser.

"Promising," I agreed. "Can't read her name. We'll have to bring the *Dolphin* over to the quay to load the crate—it'll be too big for the dinghy—and we'll take her round the cabin cruiser. Have a look-see."

Chester produced a packet of Players, and we smoked in silence for a time. The *Scillonian* was creeping up to the quay, her screw with the engines put astern, boiling the water white alongside her. It was a fine day for the trippers, and she carried a full complement, most of whom had crowded to the starboard side, giving her a list.

"Ever thought why Cookson doesn't want you in the Scillies?" Chester demanded.

"I've thought of little else since he made it plain," I said, "and I can't come up with a really satisfactory answer. He knows that I know he's a crook and that may be contributory, but I think that basically it is because I know the Islands well . . ."

"Including the uninhabited ones, eh? That don't look too good. Maybe he knows darn well that Sikes is buried on one."

"And so does Reeves-Galway. In fact I think he's bloody sure of it. Steve, it's one hell of a job. Samson is the most likely being the largest. About fifteen hundred yards north to south. Two peaks you can see from here, and the island is about a thousand yards east to west across its southern half. It's covered in bracken, bramble, and outcrops of rock. We have to find a patch six feet by two in that lot. Then there are the other and smaller islands. Annet west of St. Agnes. It's a bird sanctuary. Ever seen a puffin? Now's your chance."

Chester grinned.

"The pay's good," he reminded me.

"And no wonder," I said.

When the crowd had thinned we went over to the ship where they had started hoisting the luggage ashore on the derrick. We had no difficulty in picking out the Reeves-Galway luggage, and nobody questioned our right to help ourselves to it. The Scillies are free and easy.

There was so much of it we filled the boot and the back of the Morris.

The crate came ashore, and we left it while we ran the luggage up to the house, then returned to Holgate's where we parked to go down to the beach to the dinghy.

The *Dolphin*'s diesel started easily enough, and it was good to feel her alive under my hands on the wheel, as Chester slipped the mooring and I took her round in a wide sweep to include a close look at the cabin cruiser. Her name was *Jezebel*. She was scruffy, plain varnish over brown paint top sides, and white below the waterline; a white stained with weed. But she looked dry and watertight riding easily to her mooring.

If there was anyone aboard they were undisturbed by our close scrutiny as the *Dolphin* glided round her.

"I'll get the gen on her," Chester promised. "I was drinking in the Wolf and Bishop the other night with a bloke from Customs. He'll know about her."

The crate gave us no trouble, and although we made a point of circling the *Jezebel* again on our way back to the mooring nobody showed aboard her.

After lunch Reeves-Galway called me into the presence. He'd had a few brandies by the look of him, and was smoking a cigar. Neither the drink nor the smoke had mellowed him enough for him to ask me to sit down.

"I think," he announced slowly as if he was picking his words, "that it will be a good idea if you will take up a bodyguard role this afternoon. Young Felix has lessons with Miss Watkins till three o'clock. After that he will be free, and she will be taking him down to the beach to play. I think you ought to go along. You never know."

It was on the tip of my tongue to ask: "Never know what?" but he was watching me closely for a reaction; expecting a question. I kept silent. Instead I asked myself why it was necessary to keep an eye on the boy before Reeves-Galway had even started his grave-searching, let alone been caught at it. I was sure then that there was a great deal he knew that he was not prepared to tell Chester and me.

"It will be a pleasure," I said.

"I thought so," he nodded, and then leered at me in what was probably intended to be a man-to-man way. "She's a nice bit of stuff, eh? I wish you luck if you fancy her, Yates, but just remember that she has a job to do, and so have you. I don't think I have to worry about Chester, but you're the sort the chicks like to tumble with." He flicked the ash off his cigar. "I have the same trouble myself," he added modestly.

I stared at him. The man really meant it. I thought that any moment he would be fingering his thin black moustache like the villain in an old-time movie. I mumbled something and beat a hasty retreat.

Meg appeared with Felix in tow shortly after three. By that time Reeves-Galway and the voluptuous Lola were spread out on chaiselongues by the edge of the pool soaking in the sun. It was fairly obvious that they could not have cared less where the boy spent the rest of his day provided they were not asked to accompany him. Chester, though nominally free, was at the bottom of the garden chipping away with a hoe.

Meg had a basket with towels in it.

"I'm going to have a dip myself," she told me. "How about you?"

I had brought a pair of trunks, so I went and fetched them along with one of the household towels. Meg stowed them in the basket, and off we went spurning the transport. To stroll along the island lanes in the summer with the hedgerows on either side purple with Veronica in flower is itself a delight.

The boy whooped along in front his bare matchstick legs flashing unhealthily white in the sun.

"He's not a bad little chap," Meg remarked. "He has been thoroughly spoilt through neglect if you know what I mean. Give him anything to keep him quiet. All he needs is a firm hand."

"Which Mistress Watkins will apply, eh?"

Meg smiled, but said nothing. I was content to walk by her side. Her carriage was beautifully erect and poised. She walked like a queen.

We made for the Porth Mellon Beach because, although it was not the nearest, we knew that it was all sand, free of rock and shingle and with no cliffs behind it to be negotiated.

St. Mary's beaches are never crowded even in the season because the bulk of the visitors go out daily in the launches to the off-shore islands. We had the place to ourselves, save for half a dozen groups dotted along the stretch of near-white sand.

Master Felix was expertly stripped to a pair

of diminutive yellow trunks, and made for the water. Meg whipped off her frock and was revealed in a bikini as exiguous as that of the exotic Lola. I had to struggle into my trunks under cover of a towel and got sand in them in the process. Meg laughed.

We had a swim and I had a shot at teaching the boy, but the water was too cold for his thin body to resist. He was game enough but shivering before long. I promised to give him a lesson or two in the pool where the water was warmer.

"You'll have to keep that promise, Martin," Meg said gravely after she had rubbed the boy down and he had scampered off.

"That's been one of his troubles. Promises from Father that have never been kept. Promises lightly given to keep the boy quiet."

"I daresay. What do you think of Reeves-Galway, Meg?"

"As a father? Nothing at all. As a man," she hesitated. "Too early to give an honest opinion. Isn't it odd that we should have met after all these years, Martin?" she added brightly.

"Very," I agreed, "but delightful. Don't change the subject, Meg. What do you think of our mutual boss? Most girls can size up a man pretty quickly."

She looked at me with her big grey eyes troubled.

"I'm not being fair, Martin. I know I'm not, but I can't help it. I loathe him. He looks at me as if . . . ugh! You stare, Martin but you don't strip, if you know what I mean."

"Not much needed at the moment," I grinned, "but I know what you mean. He puzzles me, though. Listen, Meg, can you keep a confidence? Anyway, Chester knows, so why shouldn't you?"

I went on to tell her of my real purpose in getting employment with Reeves-Galway. I left nothing out.

"I remember the missing yachtsman, of course," she remarked. I had given her a cigarette during the recital, and now she drew on it thoughtfully. "Do you really think he was engaged in smuggling? Terribly difficult keeping a rendezvous in a small boat in these waters. The weather . . ."

"I know what you mean, Meg. That's what sticks in my craw. If you take a yacht out there beyond the Bishop the sea nine days out of ten would make spotting a cannister in the water a very dicey business. More often or not you would find the sea well nigh impossible on the day you'd arranged the rendezvous. Still, it is possible, especially in these days of transistors. A cannister dropped overboard could carry a tiny transmitter on which a yacht equipped with a receiver could home in any weather the yacht could sail. But what other explanation can there be?"

"Difficult," she admitted. "All I know is, Martin, that I wouldn't trust His Nibs, if I were you. I may be doing him a gross injustice, and I suppose it's only instinct, but he gives me the creeps. At lunch today I kept catching him giving me sly looks, calculating at times. I didn't like it, Martin. Once or twice he looked half crazy. La Lola watches him the whole time, and she's fearful of something. D'you think I could ask him to let me have my meals in the kitchen?"

"What about the boy, Meg? He's your charge. I can't see Reeves-Galway letting his son, even an adopted one, eat with the menials."

"I suppose not," she agreed gloomily. "Ah well. The money's good. Who am I to grumble?"

"That's what Steve Chester and I say."

Presently, when she had finished her cigarette, she went off to play with Felix. I watched her for a time. She was certainly something in her scanty green bikini, and I had to take in my thoughts a little. Yates was as fond of the ladies as the next man but he had a nice perception of how far he went with individual girls, and Meg was not the type to lead up the garden path. A great pity. But there it was. You set yourself a code and you had to keep it.

I stretched back on the sand and closed my eyes, glorying in the sun on my body. This was the life. Then a shadow fell across me, and I knew that it was not Meg's. In an instant I recalled Reeves-Galway's vague suggestion of possible trouble.

I think the man standing over me realised that his attempted annihilation was imminent before I had opened my eyes.

"Easy, Mr. Yates," he warned. "Take a look at this."

I sat up to see a small warrant in a plastic folder opened before my eyes. It carried the arms of the Duchy of Cornwall and his name in black ink. Detective Sergeant Henry Bolt.

The signature authorising the warrant was indecipherable.

"Mind if I sit down?" he asked. "Not often I get the chance of sunning myself on a Scilly beach."

"Help yourself to some sand," I said. "How do you know my name?"

"Had your description from the Met boys. Saw you leaving Coronel House. Waited till I had the chance of a word."

He was not my idea of a detective sergeant. Slight in build, and not all that tall. Untidy black hair worn too long for my taste, schooled in the Royals. A beaky nose, and brown alert eyes. He was wearing drain-pipe slacks, and a gaudy sports shirt in green and olive stripes. His feet were in fancy Italian elastic-sided shoes. He looked like the member of a pop group.

He settled down beside me, his knees drawn up and clasped in thin fingers. His eyes were on Meg's near-nude figure as she knelt beside the beginnings of Felix's sand castle.

"OK," I said, "what do you want?"

"You'd be surprised, Mr. Yates, if I told you." He grinned. "Just a joke . . . that. Nothing but a little chat. My boss,

Superintendent Trevillian, has been receiving telephone calls from Major Everard. He's a cautious man is the Super. Very sensitive to what might be going on in this corner of his manor. He sent me to check. Only three constables in the Islands, Mr. Yates. Never more than two on duty at any one time. Very tempting set-up for the criminally minded. Got anything to tell me? You looked ready to blast me for a moment. Why? Come on, Mr. Yates don't be shy," he added, when I kept silent. "What's putting you off? My appearance? What did you expect, a belted raincoat, bowler hat and size-ten regulation boots? I may look as if I should be carrying a guitar, or maybe bells and flowers, but I'm a cop. A country one perhaps, but a cop. Try me."

"How much do you know of Colonel Sikes' disappearance?"

"The lot. I've been covering the foul-play angle since it happened. If it was foul play."

He kept his gaze on Meg, who was unconsciously demonstrating how supple was her superb figure. It nettled me a little, but he wouldn't have been human had he ignored her. For a cop he was engagingly different.

"My boss, Reeves-Galway, is of the opinion

that Sikes smuggled diamonds. That his yacht was hi-jacked, that he was murdered and his body buried, not at sea because it has never been found, but on one of the uninhabited islands."

Sergeant Bolt picked up a handful of sand and let it trickle away. The silica, which gives the Scillonian beaches their near-white look, sparkled in the sunshine as it dribbled away.

"He hinted as much to me," the sergeant admitted, "but he had nothing to substantiate his suspicion that the colonel was a smuggler, or, if he had, was not prepared to give it. The idea of the body being disposed of by burial on land must have come upon him recently, presumably because it has not been washed up somewhere by the sea. Personally I think Mr. Reeves-Galway must be slightly dotty. Blokes with a great deal of money very often get queer ideas. Maybe they're entitled to them."

"Why do you think the idea is so crazy?" I demanded. "Sikes could have seen him as a potential customer. He's a millionaire."

The sergeant grabbed more sand.

"Lovely stuff," he said. "I happen to know that the Coastguard Service in these parts is extremely efficient. Sikes might have got away with it once, or even twice, but not regularly, added to which, the sea . . ."

"I know," I interrupted. "It would be hellish difficult to keep any sort of timetable to make regular rendezvous with the carrier ship, or to pick up the cargo even when it was radio plotted. But what happened to Sikes if he was not hi-jacked?"

Sergeant Bolt tore his eyes away from Meg to look at me. They were as bright as a bird's and as mischievous as a parrot's.

"They say he fell overboard, Mr. Yates. Did you hear about a renegade cop named Blagdon?"

"I did."

"Now in him I am interested. Consider the situation. In the case of Blagdon we have his body; proof that it was murdered. In the case of Sikes no body as yet. Therefore I think it could be more profitable to follow up Blagdon."

He dusted his hands fastidiously.

"You've no proof that Blagdon came to the Scillies," I said.

"No?" he demanded. "Depends what you mean by proof. The Scillonians are a tight-knit little community. They know all there is to know about each other, and about visitors who stay for any length of time. They're friendly folk. They don't mind answering questions. Blagdon was easily described. He had red hair. He stayed at the New Inn on Tresco from the 2nd July to 25th September last year. He called himself Phillips and he drank a lot of beer. He made frequent trips to St. Mary's."

The sergeant paused and his bright eyes roved across the beach from where we were sitting at its northern end to the life boat station on its little promontory and beyond to the harbour and its moored yachts.

"Blagdon was often seen aboard a yacht," he said. His thin finger pointed. "The big two-masted one. The white yawl. See her?"

"You mean Reeves-Galway's yacht, the *Dolphin*," I said.

"That's her," he agreed. "But when I asked Reeves-Galway last April—I couldn't ask him when I was here making enquiries about Blagdon because he wasn't here then—he denied all knowledge of a man called Phillips. Interesting, ain't it?"

"Very," I said. "What did you do about it?"

"Me? What could I do about it? He's a rich socialite and I'm just a country copper. I took his word for it. For the time being," he added.

The *Scillonian*'s siren suddenly blasted off which meant that she would be sailing in half an hour. The sergeant got to his feet and dusted the sand from his thin shanks.

"That's my call," he said. "Been nice meeting you, Mr. Yates. You look as though you can take care of yourself, which is a good thing. But then so did Blagdon. Six feet one and fifteen stone, he was, and look where he finished. Bysie-bye, Mr. Yates."

He looked pointedly at Meg still patting determininedly at the sides of a distinctly shaky sand castle.

"Glory be!" he exclaimed. "Some blokes have all the luck."

Then he strode lightly to the dunes behind the beach, leapt over them easily, and was gone from sight.

6

CHESTER wasted no time in making enquiries of the motor-cruiser named the *Jezebel*. He was late into dinner that night, and Mrs. Peppiat, who had finished serving in the dining room, and I had started at the kitchen table before he came in.

We gave the old lady a hand with the dishes afterwards since Annie's duties finished before dinner, and then went along to our quarters over the garage.

"She's registered in Plymouth," he told me. "Chartered to a guy named Stropp through a firm of brokers in Penzance. There's two men living aboard her. Hewson, the Customs man, thinks they may be brothers but whether they're Stropps or not he doesn't know. They're clean. Pay their dues regularly. Nothing known against them, and as far as Hewson knows they arrived two weeks ago."

"Not much help," I commented.

"Oh, I don't know," he came back. "Hugh Town is not the only harbour in the Islands.

They could have been lying off Tresco. What's the name of the harbour there?"

"New Grimsby."

His mention of Tresco started a train of thought. I told him of Sergeant Bolt.

"He claims that Blagdon was often seen aboard the *Dolphin*," I went on, "and that Reeves-Galway denied all knowledge of the man. There's something damned screwy about this whole set-up, Steve, Reeves-Galway included, and I don't like it."

"Too right," he agreed.

I had managed to phone Everard after leaving the beach, while Meg and the kid had waited for me. His reception of the news that Sikes may have been smuggling diamonds had made me wonder. Everard had described it as arrant nonsense. Even over the telephone I had detected the calm and implacable assurance of a man absolutely sure of his belief. Sikes had been his life-long friend.

"He was a man of the highest principles," he had declared, "even in the smallest matters. I was with him once in Piccadilly when it came on to rain heavily. There were no empty cabs about and we had only three hundred yards to go to the Green Park Hotel. We hopped a bus.

The conductor was upstairs when we got on and he had not come down when the time came for us to get off. Sikes left a shilling with a passenger sitting inside the door for our fares. I tell you, Martin, the idea that he was using the *Globe* for smuggling diamonds is completely untenable. Reeves-Galway ought to know better than to believe such nonsense. Do you?"

"I don't think it was possible in these waters, Charles, and you knew Sikes. But what the hell did happen to him?"

"I'm hoping you can find that out," Everard had said.

My own hope had been that the *Jezebel* would give me a lead, and now that Chester had discovered that the cabin cruiser had arrived only a fortnight ago the hope was dispelled. But I was still ready to believe that the two men who had arrived in the dinghy the previous night with the intention of putting me into the harbour had come from the *Jezebel*, nor had I any doubts about their intention. The way one of them had come aboard the *Dolphin*'s dinghy had been unmistakable. He'd not come to beg a light. Moreover Cookson had sent them. There was only one reason for that fat crook to have arrived in the Scillies, and that was profit with a capital P. If it was not diamond smuggling, or some other lucrative racket then what the hell was it? And why should Reeves-Galway have claimed Sikes to have been smuggling diamonds if indeed it was so much nonsense? I could ask him, but somehow I distrusted the man. If he was a liar I wanted to know why he was lying.

Although he had suggested that he would start his grave searching that night he made no approach to us on the subject till after dark, and then he came roaring along to our quarters yelling for us to show a leg as if he was assuming that we were automatically prepared to dodge the column. He wasn't drunk but not far off it.

"What the hell am I paying you for?" he wanted to know. "Get moving. One of you fetch a case from the hall, and the other start up the Morris. Look lively! This is an ideal night for the job. Dark as sin, and no moon till near dawn."

Chester beat me down the stairs and moved into the garage so I went along to the house wondering why he needed to take a case at all till I saw Lola, in black stretch pants and jersey, standing beside one.

"Hallo, Yeets," she purred, her dark eyes full of conspiracy as if I had called secretly to whisk her off to Gretna Green.

"Are you coming with us on the *Dolphin*?" I gasped.

"*Si*. I like sheeps. My father was fisherman, did you know? When I was girl I sailed many times. My home was in Capri. Ah, so beautiful. These islands. They do not compare."

"I daresay," I answered weakly. I wondered if she have ever gone searching for a grave on Capri.

She put a hand on my shoulder with the idea of carrying on the conversation. I think she was a girl who had to have physical contact. Her fingers began digging into my shoulder muscles and her huge eyes stared challengingly into mine.

Cripes!, I thought, she doesn't waste any time. You'll never last, Yates. Then her husband's bull-like bellow came from the concourse outside, and she dropped her hand. I picked up the case. It wasn't very heavy but I was sweating when I hefted it into the boot. I thought quickly of many things, including the beautiful statuesque Meg so cool and clean. The trouble was I *wanted* Lola, and the bitch knew it. She wanted me.

Fortunately she was in the front this time alongside her husband while Chester and I filled the back.

Reeves-Galway drove at his usual lickety-split. We charged into Hugh Town as if we had come to beat the town up.

"Jesus!" I heard Chester mutter profanely. "At this rate we shan't need the dinghy to reach the yacht."

As soon as I was on the *Dolphin*'s deck, which was already wet with dew, I noticed that there was a light aboard the *Jezebel*.

The night was as dark as any would be in the Scillies at that time of year with a thin layer of cloud hiding the stars and the little light they offered. There was a light breeze from the south-west. Out in the road the water would have a lop on it, but in the harbour it was flat save for a few ripples chuckling against the ship's hull.

Reeves-Galway called us into the saloon, and faced us across its polished table and leant on it against his hands as he peered at each of us in turn. He looked excited. His eyes had a febrile glitter.

"Right!" he declared. "Let's discuss the project. I'm convinced that Sikes' body is buried on one of the uninhabited isles. Problem is—which?"

I had in mind that Sikes' yacht had last been seen by Reeves-Galway himself sailing north towards St. Martin's, but I couldn't very well suggest we search islands round St. Martin's without revealing the fact that I had studied the subject.

"Anything known of his last movements?" I asked. "He must have been seen leaving Hugh Town . . . by the Coastguards, surely?"

"They logged him travelling towards St. Martin's, but that could have been a deliberate detour on his part to avoid being seen making for the Bishop. He could have gone out through the Beef Neck, headed north-west till he had the Bishop Light clear on his port beam, and then headed south-west. The wind was due out of the west that night. Following such a course would have given him a minimum of tacking."

"If he was hi-jacked somewhere west of the Bishop," I put in, "his yacht would not have finished up on the Seven Sisters Reef. That's for sure."

"Unless it was taken in tow and deliberately

set adrift east of the Islands," he argued, and added on a curious note, "You sound familiar with these waters, Yates?"

"I've studied the map, sir."

He gave me an evil look from his smeary eyes, and then said:

"I think he's on Samson."

Chester and I kept silent, not without effort on my part for it seemed to me that Reeves-Galway *knew* that Sikes' body was buried on Samson, and not on Tean, or English Island, or Annet, or on one or two of the tiny islets on which it would have been possible to land a body. Most of them are nothing but rocks.

Finally Chester said:

"OK, sir, make it Samson."

Reeves-Galway fetched a large-scale map, specially prepared by the look of it from an Ordnance one. Either he'd had it done for him or had drawn it himself. It seemed to me to be a further argument in favour of him being certain that Sikes was on Samson and nowhere else. How the hell did he know?

"South Hill. North Hill," he said pointing at them in turn with a pencil. "They wouldn't have wanted the labour of carting a corpse very far up a slope, so we can ignore anything above the fifty-foot contour line. The first one is twenty-five feet. There are a few flower fields on the south-eastern corner of South Hill, and that seems to me to be a likely spot. Let's get going. I'll take her over under power. You'd better break open the crate and get the tools aft into the cockpit. The tide's on the ebb and we'll have to go ashore in the dinghy."

Chester and I had dumped the crate in the forecastle through the forepeak hatch, and once we were under way we prised it open with a spike.

As I had imagined Reeves-Galway did nothing by halves. Apart from picks and shovels there were electric lamps, hand torches, and huge rolls of inch-wide white tape. These had brass ringed holes at each end and spikes for securing them to the ground. Using these methodically to tape the ground over defined areas he was not going to miss examining an inch of it. If Sikes was there we were going to find his grave. However carefully he had been buried there would be traces after three months. Bodies are uncommonly difficult to conceal even underground.

Lola, who had gone into her state-room with her case, as soon as we had gone aboard, was in the saloon pouring drinks when Chester and I took some of the lighter equipment through the saloon to the cockpit. The picks and shovels we put out on deck through the hatch.

She put a finger to her lips when she spotted us.

"Wait!" she whispered. Then she giggled, took up a large whisky she had poured, and took it through to the cockpit for her lord and master. She was back within a minute, squirming past the half-opened sliding door like a great big cat.

"Now. You boys drink, eh?" she cooed, making for the corner bar.

Neither Chester nor I found any protest. It was obvious that Reeves-Galway would never offer us one and that she had realised as much.

She sloshed out the White Label as if it was lemonade, and we toasted her.

"You know why we are going to Samson?" I asked her.

"*Si,*" she nodded, pulling a face. "I do not like it . . . looking for a body . . . ugh!"

"Your husband feels very keenly about it. Colonel Sikes was a friend of his. Were you staying at Delgardens with him when the colonel disappeared from his yacht?"

"No. I had gone back to London three days before. It was time for Felix to return to school, you know? I went with him. I did not want to go, but my husband said yes I must go."

She sipped daintily at a gin and vermouth she had poured for herself. Chester put the next question.

"Do you remember when you were staying in the Islands last year, ma'am?" he asked. "Your husband employed a big red-headed man at times to help crew this ship . . ."

"Why do you ask me about him?" she demanded, suddenly upset. She was staring at the startled Chester as if he had sprouted horns. She gripped her glass so hard I thought that its thin stem might snap. Then she shook her head vigorously.

"No. I do not remember such a man. Why do you ask? Why?"

"Sorry, ma'am," Chester mumbled humbly. "Only that I knew a feller . . ." He took refuge in his glass swallowing the whisky at a gulp.

At that moment Reeves-Galway let out a stentorian roar.

"Yates! Chester! What the hell are you doing? Get up here!"

We gathered the torches and lamps we'd

carried into the saloon and ducked up the few steps into the cockpit.

The light from the dash highlighted his features, his thin line of jet-black moustache and his gleaming white teeth clamped round a pipe stem. He had the yacht at half-speed and she was surging gently forward, dipping gracefully in the slight swell. It was as black as pitch overboard. I could hardly make out the line of the masts against the sky, though this may have been my eyes after the light in the saloon or the yacht's navigation lamps carving tiny pools of red and green out of the gloom.

"Keep watch aft," Reeves-Galway grunted. "We may be followed. You never know."

There were glasses on a rack over the helmsman's chair. I took them out of their case, focused them on the lights of the quay behind us and then swept the sea aft. If there was a bow wave trailing us I ought to have seen it, dark as it was, but in fact there was nothing.

"All clear," I reported.

"Sir!" he snarled. "You ought to know how to report, Yates."

"Sir!" I echoed savagely.

The trip took barely twenty minutes. I'll say this for Reeves-Galway. He knew those waters intimately, or he had radar for eyes. He took her in confidently with Nut Rock close to starboard, making for the channel between Green Island and Stony Island. Then he swept the *Dolphin* round the northern tip of Green Island on a reverse course into a small bay of deeper water south of Samson Flats. Chester was posted in the pulpit with a lead and we inched towards Samson till there was barely two feet of water under her keel when the anchor went down to drag till the hook caught and held us firm in dead flat water about a hundred yards off Samson's shore.

Chester and I loaded the dinghy over the stern, keeping one of the powerful hand lamps ready for use to light us ashore.

"We'll need to be careful how we use these lamps on the island," I said. "They're bright enough to be seen on Tresco. If they spot us they'll think we're a party left behind by one of the St. Mary launches."

"We'll watch it," Reeves-Galway said.

Lola had stayed in the saloon. It was my guess she was loading herself with gin for the coming expedition, for she seemed as fond of the hard stuff as her husband.

When we were ready to leave ship he went

into the saloon to fetch her. He was gone some time and we heard their voices raised in argument.

"She don't want to come," Chester suggested. "Funny how she blew up when I mentioned Blagdon."

"She was scared, Steve. It's my guess His Nibs gave her a D-notice about his employing Blagdon."

Reeves-Galway came out alone. I noticed that under one arm he was carrying the long red leather case I had last seen on the shelf of the state-room cupboard; the case with the knives. As armament, if any was required they were better than nothing but a couple of shotguns, for which he would have had no difficulty in getting a licence would have been more practical.

"My wife is not going ashore," he growled. "She will be all right on her own. Get into the dinghy, Chester, up in the bows with one of the lamps. There's rocks about at low tide. We don't want to stove her in."

Chester had scrambled over the stern of the yacht, and I was leaning over to pull the dinghy round so that Reeves-Galway and I could settle ourselves aft when I heard it; the unmistakable beat of a ship's motor. As soon as I lifted my head it was gone, blanketed perhaps by the yacht's superstructure. Then when I ducked overside again I could hear it.

"Hold it!" I said tersely. "We're not alone. There's a power boat coming in. I can hear it with my head down on the water. Wait!"

In less than a minute it was plain, a steady rhythmical beat, coming louder and louder.

Reeves-Galway grabbed the glasses and scrambled forward. I followed. Chester stayed in the dinghy.

"No lights!" Reeves-Galway was sweeping in the direction of the sound. "Douse all ours. Quickly!"

I dashed back to the cockpit, and threw off the switches, went down to the saloon to do the same. Lola was in the state-room and I banged on the door.

"Douse all lights!" I called, and not waiting for her reaction groped my way back on deck.

The beat of the motor was loud through the darkness. A diesel, I thought. At a guess she was following the same course as we had done, passing down the channel between Green and Stony Islands. If it was the *Jezebel* she could go in over Samson Flats, for she was drawing less water than the *Dolphin*.

The sound diminished and then died abruptly as she throttled down.

Lola was in the cockpit when we returned aft.

"Victor!" She clung dramatically to her husband in the darkness, "I will go with you please."

"No, my dear. Stay on the yacht. It might not be pleasant, and you will be perfectly safe here. You can go to bed."

That was odd, I thought. Chester and I had assumed that she had been unwilling to go ashore, whereas Reeves-Galway had not wanted her.

"Then leave one . . . Chester or Yeets on the sheep. I am afraid. Please, Victor."

I found myself saying,

"I'll stay for a bit, sir, if you like. I can wade ashore later. After all, that power boat might not have anything to do with us."

But it had, of course. The very fact that she had been showing no lights, and had been willing to come in close where the sailing was tricky on a low tide, were indication enough. She'd guessed our destination to be Samson and

112

it was more than likely that she had spotted our riding light high on the mast before we had doused.

A second after I had made the offer I realised my true reason for making it.

You rat, Yates, I told myself, you cheap conniving rat. You want the chance to be alone with Lola. Already I could imagine the two of us together on the settee in the saloon. In the dark, with only the feel of her to guide me. I was almost hoping he would refuse the offer and make the girl stay aboard alone.

He grunted, one leg over the stern.

"OK. But we'll need you ashore if we're going to get any worth while work done at all. Besides, they'll see our lights and if there's to be trouble they'll make it with us, not the yacht. Give you half an hour."

He got aboard while I steadied the dinghy.

"We'll have to paddle," he told Chester, meaning that Chester would while he lighted the way from the bows. They swapped places, Chester dipped the paddles, and they disappeared into the gloom with only the chuckle of water to mark their going.

Lola was in the cockpit and she came to me

as soon as I had dropped down from the counter.

"Oh, Yeets," she whispered, "I am afraid. So afraid."

I put my arms round her. She was shivering.

7

I TOOK her down into the saloon, and though the feel of her was delicious it was no time for illicit love-making. Lola was scared, and I wanted to know the reason.

I put her on one of the big settee benches along the side of the ship, then left her there.

"Where are you going?" she wailed.

"To draw the curtains," I answered. It took no time at all and when it was done I switched on the lights.

"You think I am silly woman?" she blinked up at me. The dark eyes had lost some of their fear with the coming of light.

"Not at all."

I crossed to the bar, and mixed her a stiff gin and Italian, which I judged to be her favourite tipple. I poured a whisky for myself.

I took the drink over to her and sat down beside her.

"Why are you scared?" I asked her.

She sipped the drink, and then made a little

gesture of helplessness that nearly spilled the glass.

"I am not. Not now, with you, Yeets."

Her free hand came over to touch my arm, and then the fingers began their caressing movements. I wouldn't have put it past her to have staged the whole thing. After all, she was an actress, and although she might have fooled me I didn't think she could have fooled Reeves-Galway. He wouldn't have let me stay aboard otherwise. He had known that his wife was scared. Moreover, he knew why.

"Listen," I said doggedly, "you were scared of being left alone on the yacht. Why?"

"There will be trouble, I think. Victor my husband, he is expecting it. He says that the men who killed Colonel Sikes will not let him find the grave."

"That figures," I agreed, "but you must have known that before we left the house tonight. Why did you come at all?"

"Because I did not want to be left alone in the house . . . stupid!"

She sounded if she was becoming choked with my questions. Maybe I was not reacting to the fingers dancing on my bare forearm. I was. It was as much as I could do not to put down

116

my drink and grab her. She was the sexiest bundle I had encountered in years. She pressed into me, her leg against mine. She set down her glass on the saloon table, reaching forward to do it. With another arm free she was able to put a hand on the back of my neck.

"But you would not have been alone in the house," I said firmly.

"There's Mrs. Peppiat, Miss Jenkins and the boy."

"But no men! What is the matter with you, Yeets? If the men had come to the house while you and Chester and Victor are digging on this island what could three women do? You were hired to protect us."

"Now, wait a bit," I protested. "It hasn't come to that—yet. Nor is it likely to. You're jumping to conclusions."

She jerked away from me suddenly. Her eyes flashed and she said some explosive word in Italian.

"I do not know why I try to be nice to you, Yeets. You are like all Englishmen. Love must be so respectable, eh? I sit down beside you. I rub myself against you. I caress you. And what happens? You ask me questions. Questions. Questions!"

I stood up purposefully, towering over her so that she had to bend her head back to look up at me with dilated eyes.

"I haven't finished yet Lola. Listen to me. I am not going to make love to you out of respect for your husband. Not that I have a great deal of it, either for him, or for you. But I am taking his money, and that makes a difference. Stupid English custom, eh? I want the truth about this Sikes business. I want the truth about the man your husband was employing on the yacht last year. His name was Blagdon, but he called himself Phillips while he was staying on Tresco. Are you going to tell me what you know, or am I . . ."

I paused. I was sure that I had heard the soft splash of water alongside the yacht. Yes, there it was again. As much noise as the paddles of a dinghy would make used carefully. It was going down the port side towards the stern.

"Stay here!" I hissed at the girl.

I made the cockpit once I was out of the saloon in two leaping strides, but it was as dark as hell, like diving into a barrel of ink, after the glare of the saloon.

There was a torch on a rack in the cockpit. I found it quickly enough, but by the time I had my hand on it, my mind had already guessed that the visitors were not attempting to board us. The dinghy was astern somewhere and moving away. They had been content with a quick reccy.

I switched on the torch, adjusted its focus to a long beam and sent the light probing the dark. It settled on the dinghy within seconds. It may have been the one that had called upon me the previous night; certainly it was no bigger. Now it was crowded with three men, who squashed it with their combined weight so that their backsides appeared no more than an inch above water. One was in the bows, and two were in the stern with an oar each. I didn't recognise them, and their appearance registered nothing save that they were suntanned, wearing open-necked shirts of various hues and were hefty specimens.

The man in the bows cupped his mouth with his hands and shouted.

"Ahoy, *Dolphin!* D'you hear me? Stay off Samson! Is that clear? Stay off Samson, or it will be the worse for you. Do you hear that?"

"I hear you!" I bawled back. I was tempted to add some parting shot like "Drop dead!" but since I would have had to have shouted the words they appeared ridiculously banal even as I prepared to mouth them, and I let them go unsaid.

The dinghy altered course, back to the *Jezebel*, if it was the cabin cruiser who owned her. I kept the light on her till she melted into the darkness at the end of the beam.

I was sure that Reeves-Galway and Chester must have heard the shouting, and so I flashed the shore continuously till I raised an answering series. I thought it was possible that Chester understood Morse if Reeves-Galway didn't, and flashed a message.

"Visited by three men in dinghy. Warned off Samson."

It was laborious work, for I had to rack my memory for the morse in which I had never been expert. However, the answer when it came was no more skilfully sent.

"Coming to fetch you."

Well, I was glad of that. The swim would have been nothing, but the night was cool and would be colder before dawn. The idea of searching the ground in wet pants didn't appeal to me at all.

The Evinrude spluttered, then shattered the night with its roar. Presumably secrecy had been sacrificed in the interests of speed. I kept the light going astern and presently Chester standing in the dinghy came swooping alongside.

"You know something?" he grinned, as soon as he had switched off. "You're wanted. The boss don't quit easily. In fact he's spoiling for a fight. He's got a bloody great knife stuck in his belt. I haven't seen anything like it since the Black Pirate."

His arrival had not gone unheard by Lola, who came up from the saloon as he finished talking.

"And Lola?" I asked Chester. I guessed the answer, and cursed Reeves-Galway in the same breath. Unfairly perhaps. She had probably agreed to stay on the yacht as a condition for being allowed to come at all. Still, he ought to have guessed that woman-like she would change her mind.

"I will come with you, yes?" she demanded.

"Sorry, ma'am," Chester said. "Boss's orders. You stay aboard. I'm to give you the Very pistol. Show you how to fire it. If trouble arrives you fire one red."

He had lashed the dinghy while speaking and now he came over the side. Lola's reaction was quick. She was cat-like in her movements. I think that was one of the reason's I found her so attractive physically. She was no sylph, but generously rounded, and yet she was as lithe as they come. I had kept the torch burning and all I saw was a flick of her black-clad legs as she dropped into the dinghy. She sat with her arms folded over her breasts and spat:

"Now you take me ashore!"

Chester began appealing:

"Look, ma'am . . ."

I interrupted him.

"Let her stay. I'm not sure it isn't the wisest thing. The boss will have to lump it. We can put the covers on the yacht."

Locking up took some time, and a torch was flashing angrily from the beach before we were aboard the dinghy and snorting ashore, with Lola in the bows holding a light.

I lifted her across the last few feet of water, and dumped her in front of lord and master, who swore unrestrainedly.

"You disobeyed orders," he rapped at Chester.

"He didn't have the option," I put in. "Your wife has a mind of her own, or hadn't you noticed? Besides, she's better off with us than left alone on the yacht."

"They can help themselves to the yawl while she's unprotected."

"So they can, but what good will it do them? She'd only be an embarrassment. Your yacht is known all over the Islands."

He glared at me in the bright light of the lamps. As Chester had said, Reeves-Galway had stuck one of his fancy knives into the belt of his slacks, and now he had one hand lightly on its haft.

"I don't like your tone, Yates. You don't show enough respect."

If Lola had not been standing there, still hugging herself, I would have given him a very rude word indeed, and to hell with his money. I was getting thoroughly choked with Reeves-Galway, and the prospect of spending the remainder of the night hunting for a grave that in all probability would demand a number of nights before it was found. The man's attitude was ridiculous; so indeed was his stance. Legs wide apart, hand on knife as if he was King of the Castle.

"Let's get cracking," he went on impatiently when I made no reply. "I've chosen a plot in the first of the fields. We'll put a tape across, search the ground along it, then put down another using the first as a marker. When we've searched the second we'll lift the first using the second as a marker. We'll go on like that for the length of the field. Get it?"

Chester had already taken the tools off the beach to the chosen spot, and we moved off in a bunch. Lola, I think wanted to take her husband's arm. She had to have contact. But he shook her off. At least that was my impression for the two of them moved off in front of us, Reeves-Galway having picked up a lamp, but Chester switched off his light just as she was reaching for hubby's arm.

There is a bridle path that encircles the entire periphery of Samson and we moved left along this as soon as we were off the beach. South Hill loomed above us on the right, a shade blacker than the cloud-covered sky.

The fields in the Scillies are small by design, and protected by high hedges, mostly of Veronica, used as windshields to give shelter to the spring flowers they grow. In June the fields are empty, some tilled, others lying covered in grass and weed which they burn off later before replanting the bulbs. I had not been on Samson for years, and whether or not these few fields were still being worked by the folk from Bryher or Tresco I never learnt. The first one we reached through a broken-down gate in its high hedge was covered in grass and weed. If anybody had buried Sikes's body in it he would have needed to be a genius not to have left traces. I suspected that the sub-soil was sand, and below that solid rock but how far one dug to reach it was anyone's guess.

Chester held a tape, while I walked across the bottom of the hedge, drew it taut and spiked it to the ground. Reeves-Galway got Lola to hold another and came across it with it keeping it two yards from mine, and spiked that. It was quite a system, and it was surprising how quickly we could work even in the dark. While he and I scrutinised the ground between the tapes Lola and Chester stretched out another between them.

At the top of the field Reeves-Galway fell us out for a smoke and a nip.

The elevation was higher here, above the twenty-five contour on his map, and although I could get a shrewd idea of where the beach ended and the sea began by a faint phosphorescent glow from the tiny waves lapping the sand, I could not make out the yawl.

"What about the opposition?" I asked the boss.

"What about them?" he returned. "I hope they arrive, Yates. We shall teach them a lesson in no uncertain fashion."

"Perhaps," I said. "Suppose they're armed?"

He drew fiercely on the Perfecto he had lit and its red glow reflected from the sweat on his face. I could see his mouth with its hairline moustache. It looked cruel, and there was a line to his jaw that suggested the obstinacy of a mule.

"I'd like that," he said throatily. "My word, I would. Guns would be little use to them in the dark. I fancy the idea of stalking an armed man, getting up close to him and spitting him with a knife."

He laughed and it could have been the greatest prospective joy in the world to judge from his cackle.

"I'm pretty sure that the motor we heard came from a cabin cruiser called the *Jezebel*," I said. "She's been moored in the harbour at Hugh Town for a fortnight. It suggests that they have been waiting for you; keeping an eye

126

on the *Dolphin*; waiting for you to move. Agreed?"

"If you say so, Yates."

"Then it is obvious that they have known for some time that you proposed searching for Sikes' body on Samson. How did they learn of it?"

"I haven't the remotest idea," he returned lightly.

"But I have," I came back at him forcibly. "They *know* the body is on Samson, possibly because they buried it here. They also know that you are aware of it. They're not out here in force because they fear an inspired guess on your part might lead you to finding the body. You *know* it's on Samson, don't you—sir?"

I added the sir after an insulting pause and I could feel his hackles rising.

"You're not paid to ask questions, Yates. You're paid to do as I tell you. If you don't want the job you can jack it in when you like. Get on the first helicopter tomorrow."

He was boiling inside himself, I could tell. He stuck the half-smoked cigarette into his mouth and drew on it so fiercely it should have burst into flame. I was tempted to take him at his word. Then I thought of Everard, who

127

would have called it failure on my part, though he wouldn't have said so, and I also thought of Meg, oddly enough.

"For Pete's sake!" I said aloud. "I'm sorry. I'm only trying to help. But be reasonable. It's fairly damned obvious that you know Sikes is on the island. You've even had a large-scale map prepared. If you'll tell me what really happened then maybe I can be of some proper use to you."

He was quiet for a bit. Farther along, Chester and Lola were saying nothing, just squatting side by side smoking. They must have heard every word of the conversation, for we were on the lee side of the island, and the air was almost still.

"Yates," Reeves-Galway pronounced, tearing each word out of his throat, "the only help I want from you is to obey orders. Will you get that into your thick head? Do as I say or clear out!"

I was swallowing this the best I could when we heard the sound of a ship's motor start up. From its direction it was undoubtedly the *Jezebel*. It grew louder as we followed the sound and strove to penetrate the darkness for a sight of her. It came abreast, passed us and then died away to a faint murmur till it was lost against the soft splash of the sea on the beach.

"Gone home!" Reeves-Galway sneered. "So much for the opposition. Come on, let's get to work."

He drove us as if we were a chain gang. His whole attitude suggested that having cowed the enemy by showing them that he was undeterred by threats he was going to find Sikes' body that very night. He didn't. We laboured for two hours, including Lola, who was making it obvious that she wanted to return to the yawl with every step that she took, then he called a halt.

We all returned to the *Dolphin*, where Lola brewed coffee. There was still an hour to daylight when we had finished the hot drink, and Reeves-Galway ordered us back in the dinghy.

Lola stayed aboard.

His idea, he said, when we were on the beach again was to finish searching the fields that night. I remember thinking then that I hoped we found the body of Sikes. I was beginning to regard the missing colonel with almost as much dislike as I did the millionaire playboy who was so intent on finding him.

The sky was lightening perceptibly in the east when we reached the last field high up on South Hill. I could see the bracken on the slope above us, grey in the dawn light. By the time we had spread the tapes to and fro across the weed-strewn patch between the Veronica hedges, colour had crept back into the world.

The attack came as we prepared to reel in the last tape having found nothing. It was heralded by a shrill whistle and four men leapt out of the bracken where they had lain concealed, and converged on us in a swift and rather sinister silence. Each carried a cosh of sorts.

I recall Chester saying: "Christ!" and Reeves-Galway making a sort of throaty growling noise. He had discarded his knife earlier, because a great deal of stooping had been necessary in the search and his swashbuckling way of carrying it stuck in his belt had been uncomfortable. His unarmed combat was not all that hot, however, because he was the first to go down.

The attacking squad, who had obviously been left behind by the *Jezebel* and had waited in the bracken till they had sufficient daylight to see by, had exercised a disciplined patience till they broke cover. Then they blundered for they failed to pick an individual target. That was my impression. Maybe they had each been instructed to make Reeves-Galway the first target, or perhaps they were chilled and cramped by their long wait in the dew-soaked bracken. At any rate they seemed to slow down as they reached us, and the first blows with the coshes which were to have knocked us silly seemed ponderous.

I picked a man on their left flank who was actually wielding a policeman's truncheon. In the split second before I moved it looked as if he was aiming at Reeves-Galway, who was between Chester and me. I went flat on my back and brought up my right foot, clad, unfortunately, in a rubber-soled canvas shoe and not an ammunition boot, and kicked him accurately in the groin. He doubled up. I came off the ground and gave him a couple of Karate chops to the neck, and he pitched on to the spot I had so lately left.

The truncheon was thonged to his hand and there was no time to free it for personal use. Reeves-Galway was down, but he seemed to have given one of them something to think about, for he was standing off, just looking at him. His mate, however, was stepping in with a long rubber cosh coming back high. I could see the whip in the thing as he brought it back. I hurled myself at him, going for his cosh arm. The motion brought the two of us down sliding into the soft earth of the field. But I kept my grip on his arm, turned it into a lock, and put on the pressure. The ulna broke with a perceptible crack and its owner screamed. I let him go.

Chester was having a stand-up fight with his man. Each time the fellow tried to get in a blow with his cosh Chester cracked him a right or a left to his face with a boxer's precision, without being able to put him down. The man's nose was streaming blood.

I ought not have spared a glance at Chester. The fellow who had first coshed Reeves-Galway, and who had been standing off to admire his handiwork while his mate finished it, was charging in. I was late moving and his rubber cosh caught me on the left shoulder. It was numbed for a moment and then felt as if a red-hot iron had been applied. The man was a big sweaty number with sparse sandy hair and a paunch into which I sank my right fist with all the speed I could muster, grunting almost as much with the effort as he did on receiving it. He was game. He wanted to stay on his feet, and he succeeded, but all the wind had been driven out of him, and he doubled up slowly, his big red face coming down as if he were bowing with respect. I waited, intent on the timing, and then snapped up my right knee. It caught him on the mouth and he toppled over sideways, still with the kind of slow dignity that seemed part of him.

Before he reached the earth a whistle was sounding urgent blasts from the bracken above us. This was evidently an unseen boss—Cookson?—sounding the retreat. Its curative effect was magical. Chester's man broke it off immediately, leaping away as if possessed. The first man I had downed had got groggily to his feet, and to give him his due was about to pitch in again. He swore fruitily at me, turned, and ran. The one with the broken arm, which he hugged with his sound left, went with him. Even Fatso turned over like a barrel, crawled for a little way, then staggered to his feet in their wake.

"Well, what d'ya know?" Chester gasped.

It was victory, but for how long? They would return if we returned. The next time they would be properly armed. The prospect brought me no joy. There was too much scope for lawlessness on an uninhabited island. Reeves-Galway had proved his point. I was ready to believe now that Sikes had been buried on the island and the police if they were informed of the night's happenings would be ready to believe it as well. They should now be told. A telephone call to the mainland would bring them in numbers. But I was fairly sure that Reeves-Galway would not have them at any price.

He was sitting up rubbing the side of his head and looking dazed. Then he came to his senses and stood up. The retreating forces were tracking away through the bracken towards the middle of the island, probably to rendezvous with the *Jezebel*, if she was not already waiting having returned to the island by a circuitous route to avoid our hearing her motor.

"After them!" Reeves-Galway screeched.

"Oh, for Pete's sake!" I groaned.

"Let 'em go, sir." Chester urged. "They won't come back in a hurry."

Reeves-Galway glared at us, swore horribly, and then charged down to the bottom of the field where he had left jackets and the greater part of the equipment.

"What the hell's got into him?" Chester asked.

"I'm damned if I know," I answered. Then, "Cripes! He's gone for a knife. Come on Steve. We've got to stop him. This has gone far enough."

As we charged down the field towards him I saw him drop the case from which he had taken one of the knives. He glanced at us, hesitated, yelled. "Come on!" and then ran through the gateway into the field down towards the bridle path above the beach. His plan was obvious. Travelling along the smooth turf of the path he would move four times as fast as the men he was after, who sooner or later, would have to come down to the path and cross it to reach the beach.

He didn't think that we were actually in pursuit of him to stop him or we would never have caught him. He sprinted off at a tremendous speed like a stag with hounds on his tail. Then he paused to turn and shout at us.

"Come on, you bastards! What's holding you back?"

I realised that argument would be useless and as soon as I was level with him I went for the knife, and disarmed him, using a grip that made it drop from his nerveless fingers.

"Don't be a bloody fool," was all I said.

He went beserk. He choked with rage and frustration, lashed out at me, with his eyes bulging and his teeth showing like an animal's. Chester got round behind him, while I dodged, then put both his arms round him at the shoulders, slid his own down to lock them in front, and neatly tipped Reeves-Galway on to his back. I helped hold him down while he sobbed with fury, calling us the filthiest names he could find.

He quietened down at last.

Chester was apologetic.

"Sorry about this, sir," he kept saying, "but if you carved up those blokes we could be in real trouble. You're not yourself."

"OK," Reeves-Galway muttered, "I'm sorry. Must be the knock on the head they gave me. I . . . I would have liked to have put a real scare into them, though."

We let him go. Indeed we helped him to his feet.

"Perhaps it was just as well you stopped me, eh?" he asked, looking suddenly sly. "Let's go home. I could do with some breakfast."

While we were gathering the equipment to load into the dinghy Chester managed a word aside with me. His blue eyes were worried.

"Did you see how he *looked?*" he demanded. "His eyes, I mean? Gave me the creeps. He was like a madman!"

8

WE slept till lunchtime. I awoke to find that the cloud of the previous night had disappeared, and that it was another blazing day. My shoulder where the cosh had caught it was as sore as hell and turning blue. After a shower, however, and then the rubbing in of an ointment that Chester produced, it felt a great deal easier. I would still be able to use the arm effectively if called upon to do so, and something told me that I would before long.

After lunch Reeves-Galway called Chester and me into the presence. He had a typewritten letter on the desk in front of him. He picked it up and waved it at us as we fell in before the desk.

"Threatening letter by the morning's post," he announced. "We tighten all security."

The man was almost jubilant about it. He seemed unaffected by the blow on the head he'd taken, but when I looked at him keenly I could see his side hair bulging over a bruise that must have been as big as a pigeon's egg.

"What does it say?" I asked.

"Stay off Samson, or else . . ." he answered.

"Nothing specific?"

He slammed the letter down on the desk.

"Listen, Yates. My words with you last night were not idle ones. Either stay quiet and obey orders or clear out. I knew this was coming. I anticipated it, which was why I hired you and Chester on the mainland. You're bodyguards. To judge by last night's performance you're damned good ones. OK! That's fine. Keep it that way. But I'm in command. I give the orders, and I don't want them questioned. Is that clear?"

During this tirade I had been squinting at the letter. There was a lot more on it than "Clear off Samson, or else . . ." It was one long paragraph in type, unsigned.

I managed to say for the sake of Everard:

"I beg your pardon."

He grunted.

"This afternoon you'll accompany Miss Watkins and the boy in whatever they happen to be doing. My wife and I will be shopping in Hugh Town, and Chester will come with us."

"Are you going over to Samson again tonight, sir?" Chester wanted to know.

"Of course. I may have to change our tactics in the light of further threats, but we'll go. For instance, we won't cross in the *Dolphin* if I can get hold of another boat. There are quite a few speed boats in the Islands. Might be able to pick up one of those, eh?"

"What's wrong with putting the whole business in the hands of the police?" I asked. "Last night's attempt to stop us looking again for a grave is pretty good proof that there's one on the island. Let them find it."

"Police?" he echoed, rather as if I had suggested the Boy Scouts. "Who the hell wants the police to do it? *I* am going to find the grave. Besides, I don't suppose there are more than a couple of bobbies in the whole of the Scillies. On top of that they would bring in a flood of reporters. No thanks, Yates. When we find Sikes they can have him on a platter, and I'll be off in the *Dolphin* for a cruise to France and back while the excitement dies down."

Three o'clock found me joining Meg Watkins and the boy for another trip to the Porth Mellon Beach. While Felix scampered ahead I told her about the previous night's shennanigans on Samson.

Meg was silent for a time after my recital and then she said:

"I don't quite get it, Martin. There's something a bit illogical about this private war over a grave, don't you think? Supposing Cookson's mob, if you can call them that, did kill Sikes and bury him on Samson . . ."

"And that's illogical in itself," I put in, "for they must have taken the trouble to sail him to Samson after they had killed him at sea, had all the bother of landing a corpse and then burying it, when all they had to do was to tip him overside in deep water. Granted somebody, perhaps the same crowd, did precisely that with Blagdon's corpse and he let them down by breaking loose from his moorings, they would surely have been guided by experience and made sure that Sikes didn't come up, rather than go to the extraordinary lengths they did. It doesn't make sense."

"No," Meg agreed, "nor does it make sense that they should bother to engage in a pitched battle to stop Reeves-Galway finding the grave. What if he does find it? There's not a shred of proof to suggest that they put the body in it.

Why should they worry? In fact they have now drawn attention to the fact that they know all about it, of which everybody was ignorant till last night."

She stopped and stared at me with wide eyes.

"Martin, do you think it possible that both parties know that Sikes is buried on Samson but neither party knows where? Maybe there is something buried with him which both want."

"You mean . . . diamonds? That he was in fact a smuggler?"

"What else?"

"I'm damned if I know," I answered after a pause, and meant it.

She took my arm when we moved off, and presently she said:

"Martin, I don't think I'm going to last long in this job."

"That makes two of us," I grinned. "I've been invited to catch the first helicopter half a dozen times already."

We both burst out laughing. It really was impossible to remain serious for long in such glorious surroundings.

"You know," she said after a time, when we were approaching the beach, "His Nibs plans a long cruise in the *Dolphin* within a day or two.

He was talking about it at lunch. We are all expected to go, with the exception of Mrs. Peppiat. I'm not sure that I want to."

"Why not? Sailing doesn't worry you, Meg. You've been brought up in boats."

"Two things. I don't think it will be a cruise in the accepted sense. I think he plans to *live* aboard the yawl, pottering round the Islands by day, and returning to Samson for his wretched grave searching at night. That way he won't be so vulnerable to attack. Next, I don't want to be in close contact with Reeves-Galway all day and night on a small ship."

It was my turn to stop and stare.

"Meg," I demanded fiercely, "has that so-and-so made a pass at you?"

She pretended to treat it lightly by giving the question a mock consideration before replying:

"M'm! Not exactly. But he's given every sign that he will before long."

"Christ!" I swore bitterly. "That will be the last straw. He can have my job if he does, and a poke in the jaw as well."

Meg stood off and regarded me gravely. Then she smiled.

"You really mean that, Martin, don't you? Nice to have a champion." She giggled. "Sorry,

I've just remembered what a loathsome lout I used to think you were as a schoolboy."

At that moment young Felix came trotting back to demand that we get a move on, impatient to be playing around on the beach.

Proceedings followed the same pattern, only this time I had taken care to don trunks before leaving the house. We had our swim, and while the boy scampered off Meg and I lay back on the sand to let the sun dry us.

A voice I recognised came from behind us.

"Mind if I join you?"

I sat up abruptly. Things were indeed following the same pattern.

"Detective Sergeant Henry Bolt," I told Meg. He came down off the dunes. He was dressed exactly as he had been yesterday, and it was difficulty to believe that he had left St. Mary's slept in his own bed, and returned that morning. I waved a hand.

"The beach is free."

He paused before sitting down to look pointedly at my bruised shoulder. He made clicking noises of disapproval.

"Nasty bruise that, Mr. Yates. It's my guess it was made by what the police call a blunt instrument."

"Is this a daily pilgrimage of yours?" I asked ignoring the remark.

He squatted down. I introduced the girl and he nodded pleasantly.

"Not exactly a pilgrimage; more in the line of duty. I came in on the chopper this morning. Can't always get a seat, you know. Got to go back on the *Scillonian*. I've been over to Tresco."

"A beautiful island," I said. "Make sure you see the Abbey Gardens some time."

He picked up his handful of sand and let it trickle sparkling in the sun.

"Fair amount of speculation going on amongst the locals in New Grimsby this morning. Ships without riding lights moving off Samson, but lights flashing on the island. The parties left at dawn. Find anything, Mr. Yates? One of the ships was the *Dolphin*."

"I told you Reeves-Galway considers Sikes to have been buried on an uninhabited island, Sergeant. He plumped for Samson. We looked but found nothing. Certain vile fellows of the rabble did their best to discourage us going again. Hence this bruise."

"The brothers Sprott," he said, "in company

with Ike Tremaine and Bartholomew Gurney at present living on the cabin cruiser *Jezebel*."

"You're well clued up, Sergeant," Meg put in.

"Not really, miss. Gentlemen from my own parish. We keep tabs on 'em. If you added up all the days of honest work that bunch have done between them it wouldn't amount to more than a week. On the other hand their total time spent in prison would come out at about forty years."

"They look fair to adding to that," I grinned. "Who's employing them, Sergeant?"

He tossed what was left of his sand in the air and dusted his hands together with a dry rustling sound.

"I'm not sure of that, Mr. Yates. At one time I thought it was the same gentleman who's employing you."

I laughed.

"Whatever gave you that idea? One of them clouted him on the head this morning before dawn."

"Does he want to prefer charges?"

"Reeves-Galway?" I asked. "You're joking! He'll settle his own score. The police would bring him publicity. As a matter of fact I doubt

146

if he'll bother to inform you if he finds Sikes' body."

The sergeant laughed. His sharp little eyes danced with merriment.

"He won't find Sikes," he declared. "He's twenty fathoms down."

"Then why are those men trying to stop him finding Sikes' grave?" Meg demanded, leaning forward the better to see Bolt.

"I dunno, miss," he said.

I dug savagely at the sand with a bare heel so that it banked up against the sole of my foot.

"What the hell *does* go on here, Sergeant?" I asked. "I'm pretty sure that Reeves-Galway *knows* that Sikes is on Samson. He's mapped the island. He's devised a way of inspecting the ground by using tapes so that he won't miss an inch of it. A man doesn't do all that on a hunch. He *knows*. After all, there are countless other islands . . ."

"Sure! The ancients even buried their dead on the top of Round Island. I ask you! A pinnacle of rock stricking up out of the Atlantic a hundred and thirty feet high. How did they get 'em up there? Workmen found the tombs when they built the lighthouse. Did you know that?"

147

"I knew it," I sighed. "Listen, Sergeant . . ."

But Bolt had gone off graves.

"Are you employed by Mr. Reeves-Galway as well, miss?" he asked, leaning across me to speak to Meg.

"Of course. I'm a sort of governess to Felix, his son there."

Sergeant Bolt regarded the boy without enthusiasm.

"Skinny, ain't he? He's adopted. Did you know that?"

"You're well informed," I said.

"Sure. I know a lot about Mr. Reeves-Galway, and I'm learning more every day. He's been around. You ever heard of L'Hôpital de Grise in Switzerland? Not far from Geneva."

"What on earth . . . ?" Meg began, when the wail of the *Scillonian*'s fog-horn cut her off.

"Thar she blows!" the sergeant exclaimed. "The half-hour signal." He got to his feet in one smooth movement. "Be seeing you!"

He took a pace towards the sandhills behind us then paused.

"Watch your step, Mr. Yates. I mean that. You too, miss. The number of the local cop shop is Scillonia 999. They'll relay any message to me. So long!"

He was gone, and Meg said:

"Martin, what was all that about? I mean . . . L'Hôpital de Grise?"

I settled back on the sand.

"Make a note to remind me to find out. Bolt's no fool, Meg. I think he has a line on what's been happening out here, and it has nothing to do with Sikes smuggling diamonds. I'll talk it over with Everard when I get the chance. I'm getting a few ideas myself, and frankly, I don't like 'em."

"Such as?"

"Later," I said sleepily. "I didn't get to bed till after breakfast this morning, and a doze in the sun is my immediate objective."

"You'll blister," she forecast. She took a look round then flopped back beside me.

I slept. For how long I didn't know but I awoke to Meg's clutch on my arm.

"Martin! Wake up! Where's Felix?"

I scrabbled myself awake. The beach was blinding under the afternoon sun to freshly opened eyes and I had to shade them as I scanned the long crescent of white sand. Four small boys in separate parties but no Felix in his yellow pants.

Meg was on her feet and I followed suit. There is a small car park behind the Porth Mellon Beach; nothing but a flat stretch of concrete bordered by the road on one side and the low heaps of sand, grown with long scrubby grass, separating it from the beach.

I leapt up and across the sandhills and heard the boy scream as I moved. I was in time to see him being bundled into the back of an old Austin, which had been turned facing the way out. Even as I charged towards it, the car accelerated away. It went right which would take it up the hill, past the school, and then into the town.

Meg was shocked. There were tears in her eyes, and she trembled a little as she stood helpless amongst the sandhills.

"Oh, Martin!" she wailed.

I took her arm.

"They won't harm him, and they can't go far on the island. Get dressed, Meg. Then we'll move."

She flung her frock over her head ignoring the wet bikini, and I had to put up with wet trunks under my slacks. Shoes were more important.

Hand in hand we ran off the beach, out on to the road, and up the hill towards the school. The road forks there. Hugh Town is built on a narrow isthmus, between the bulk of St. Mary's and Garrison, almost an island on its own. The Dismal Johnnies foretell that one day the sea will come in over most of the town. The left fork as we were running is the road which leads past the Parish Church, up the hill towards the island's generating station and the hospital and dips down to run along the back of Old Town Bay and Old Town. After that it carries on to the T-junction where Reeves-Galway's driving had scared me the morning we had arrived as we had swooped down the hill from the airport. From that point onwards there is access to any of the island's roads, except those in Hugh Town and the one round Garrison.

"They must have been making for the airport," Meg gasped.

"I don't think so," I said and dragged her to a halt. We had a clear view of the harbour and its moored yachts. The *Scillonian* had cast off and was moving away stern first. I was not interested in her and my eyes sought the

Jezebel. She was there at her mooring about two cable lengths from the *Dolphin*.

"It's my guess they'll take him aboard the *Jezebel*," I told the girl. "Work it out, Meg. They'd never get him aboard a helicopter if they'd planned to take him to the mainland . . . not at this time of the year . . . and the *Scillonian* has cast off. They have to *keep* the kid somewhere."

"An empty house?" she suggested.

"Are there any on the island?"

"Well, not exactly empty perhaps, but not being used. Quite a few belong to wealthy mainlanders who only spend a month here."

"I still think they'll take him aboard the *Jezebel*."

"In broad daylight and screaming his head off?"

"Meg, my dear, this may sound callous, but he will have stopped yelling a few seconds after they had him in the car. They'll drug him, shove him in a sack, and hoist him aboard from the dinghy. I don't think they know I saw him being bundled into the car. We can afford to watch the *Jezebel* for a minute or two."

"Martin," she wailed. "The poor little devil will be terrified. We *must* do something."

"Watch!" I said. "There's a dinghy going out now. Two men in it."

The distance was too great to make out details, and it was a powered dinghy. I could hear the thin buzz of its two-stroke outboard. As far as I knew the *Jezebel*'s dinghy had no motor.

Then Meg gripped my arm.

"Martin! It is! It's making for the *Jezebel*!"

I could scarcely believe my eyes or think that my prediction would be so swiftly fulfilled. I heard the dinghy's motor die away and saw her drift towards the *Jezebel*'s ugly shape. They lashed up, and one of the men scrambled aboard. Then he leant overside, and carefully the man in the dinghy handed him what looked like a large sack, which was drawn gently inboard.

"Come on!" yelled Meg. "We've got to get out there before they lift anchor!"

This was more than we could achieve if they had planned to leave immediately, but we tore swiftly down the hill to run along the promenade behind the town's north beach towards the spot where the *Dolphin*'s dinghy had been drawn up on the sand.

Meg helped me get the craft into the water,

153

and showed every sign of scrambling aboard when I snapped:.

"Stay here, Meg! These boys play rough. Reeves-Galway and Chester are shopping in the town. Find them and tell them what's happened."

With that I lugged on the starting cord, the Evinrude fired, I gave her full throttle and surged seawards standing in the stern.

The run took barely three minutes. I shut off the throttle and glided alongside, hitched on and stood up on the *Jezebel*'s dirty deck. I spared a glance at the beach to see Meg still there watching me. I waved a hand and dropped lightly down into the ship's open cockpit. If I'd not seen their dinghy alongside from which two men had gone aboard with a sack I would have sworn the ship was empty. The hatch to the saloon was closed and there was no sound except the lap of the tide against her hull.

I slid open the hatch, dropped down the short companion way and into the saloon. There were three of them seated at the saloon's table, which still remained uncleared after a meal, but which was dominated by a large sack that had been dumped there regardless. Its open end was towards me and a number of potatoes had rolled out to add to the general clutter. I recognised the three men as the mob who had attacked us on Samson. The one whose arm I had broken was missing.

The hatch slammed to behind me and I realised that he was present, with his right arm in a sling. He had been waiting for me to enter.

The sound of the hatch going home acted as a signal. They bellowed with laughter, though none of it showed in their eyes.

"Have a spud, mate," one of them invited.

I knew then that the whole thing had been planned to get me aboard, and that the kid must be ashore still. All right, I'd boobed, but they were not going to hold me without a fight for the privilege. Nor, obviously, did they expect anything else.

I thought immediately that the one with the broken wing who had closed up the saloon's entrance behind me, was the imminent menace, and so he was. The sap was coming down even as I turned. He was not so fast with his left hand. I caught it, ducked into him and pitched him along the length of the table. His right arm had been expertly splinted but he let out a screech of pain as he thudded down on the potato sack. Unfortunately the cosh was looped to his wrist. In that confined space I was severely handicapped.

They came at me in a bunch sliding along the ship's sides out of their chairs and launching themselves simultaneously one from the front and one from each side with an admirable timing.

It didn't last long. Fatso was in front. His mouth was swollen from the punishment he'd taken that morning. I let him have another on the chin that put him on the table along with his mate and the potatoes. Then a cosh exploded over my right ear like a volcano bursting and I lost interest.

9

MY watch was in Meg's basket, so I had no idea of how long I had been out when I came to. Unconsciousness is just a blank in the mind. As soon as I had recovered sufficiently to think I could recall the blinding light of the cosh striking home, and then I was half sitting, half lying, on a sprawl of rope in the *Jezebel*'s forepeak.

Before I reached that stage, however, recovery was slow and painful with spells of nausea that left me shaking with weakness. The *Jezebel* was at sea, and that didn't help. She was pitching into a pretty good lop, and the waves were crashing against her bows. Squatting in the forepeak with a damaged head everyone of them sounded like thunder. Occasionally when the gulfs between the swell matched her length the *Jezebel* would drop abruptly with a shattering crash that rattled every loose object aboard, and she had plenty including my aching head.

The only light in the forepeak was a trickle

of daylight coming through the hawserholes, but that, added to the chill, was enough for me to realise fairly quickly that they'd stripped me down to my bathing trunks.

I thought I knew what this portended, and I didn't like it over much. I started casting round for a weapon of sorts with which to make a last fling if the opportunity came, but apart from rope and chain, in lengths too long to be of use, and a few big empty cans of paint there was nothing to wield.

I waited in complete misery, and hoped that Meg had gone into action. It might have taken her some time to find Reeves-Galway. I thought it was safe to assume, though perhaps it was no more than hope, that he was following in the *Dolphin*, for as far as he knew his boy was aboard the *Jezebel*, and he was the type to go into action himself rather than wait for the local bobbies.

The light was failing when eventually the hatch into the forepeak was suddenly pulled across with a protesting screech, and the three able-bodied ones piled swiftly in one after the other, all expecting trouble by the look of them.

"You flatter me," I said. "I'll come quietly."

"You'd better. Time's up, mate. You're

going overside. It's a long swim to shore. If you make it then I'm a monkey's uncle."

"There's a strong resemblance now," I commented.

They grabbed me and shoved me none too gently into the saloon. The table had been cleared. My anxious eyes could see nothing faintly like a weapon; no table knives, nor bottles, nor even a jug. The fellow with the broken arm was obviously in the cockpit at the wheel.

"Can't we talk this over?" I asked at random. "After all you're four tagged men. You need to be careful. Messrs Tremaine, Gurney, and the brothers Sprott. How much is Cookson paying you for this little charade? Or, rather, how much has he *promised* you? There's a difference."

I was being propelled through the saloon towards the cockpit and the effect made them pause in their efforts. They'd not liked being named.

The fat one seemed to be acting spokesman though whether or not this made him in command I couldn't tell. I thought there was a resemblance between the one holding my left arm, and the one I had damaged, who was now

outside at the wheel. Both were as dark as Span-
iards, a quality often found in Cornishmen.
This could have made them the brothers Sprott.

Fatso came round to the front of me.

"You must be Gurney," I guessed.

For answer he brought up his fist, balled like
an outsized grape fruit, slap at my mouth. I saw
it coming and moved enough to take it on my
cheek. I swung a foot upwards, but they'd
anticipated the move and drew me back so that
I kicked air.

"You're learning fast," I said. "I made you
an offer. How much is Cookson paying you?"

"More than you can match, Yates—the
racket he's working. What are you worth
anyway? Bleedin' ex-officer on his beam ends.
That's all you are. I'll tell you somethin'. You
can thank your lucky stars Cookson wants you
found drowned, and not roughed up, or, by
Christ, you'd remember the names of Gurney,
Sprott and Tremaine when you're down in hell!
Get him up topsides, boys!"

The *Jezebel* was still dipping and rising like
a flatulent duck when we stumbled into the
cockpit. It was evening and the sun was low
enough on the horizon to play hide and seek
behind the long swell. The ship was heading

south and it was my guess we were outside the Western Isles. I had time to cast a wild look round; a frantic searching look that saw little but a confused mass of lopping green water. As they grabbed me and pitched me over the port quarter I thought I caught a glimpse of a tiny red sail way over north. It was gone in a moment as the waves tossed up, and then I was in the sea, frighteningly alone in a fraction of time.

The water was cold. It always is in the Scillies. A submarine earthquake way back in the early twenties played tricks with the Gulf Stream, though they say there is still one beach on Bryher where it touches warm. The reflection brought me little comfort. The sea was cold enough. I had no qualms about my ability to stay afloat for hours. The swell was worrying. It rocketed me upwards and then dropped me into the trough as if I was riding some crazy switchback, but the water was unbroken. It was the cold that would kill me.

On the top of the swell I saw the *Jezebel* going round in a long sweep. The bastards waved to me. I got myself orientated when I saw the Bishop. It was hell of a way north-west of me. They'd made certain that no lighthouse man saw their jettisoning act, but the tide, I thought must still be on the make. They'd probably had orders to wait till the turn and grown impatient. It might help.

There didn't seem to be any object in swimming. Swim where, for Crissakes? I thought. It was better to conserve my energy by doing no more than staying afloat. Or was it? That way the cold would kill me more quickly. Swimming might keep me warm but exhaust me. Heads the sea won. Tails I lost.

In the trough of the waves it was growing dark and the water reared above me black and menacing. On the crest it was green tinged with gold from the reddening sky. The Bishop was flashing now, occulting white, as they said in the guide books. To me it was a derisive twinkle that heightened to a glare for a fraction of a second. I looked for the flashing white of Peninnis Head, but I never saw it. I thought St. Agnes must be in the way though I could not see it during the short time the sea boosted me high on a wave top. The eastern sky was darkening and I could see no land against it. There are a few houses on St. Agnes whose lighted windows face west which I might have seen. It meant, probably that I was too far off the island. The lighthouse there, so prominent by day, is no longer in use.

When the cold gripped me I swam vigorously, and fell into a pattern. Swim. Float. Swim again. But at the end of each spell I was colder; much colder, feet and arms threatening to become numbed.

I began thinking desperately of my chances of making one of the Western Isles. Rocks mostly, with only a ghost of a chance of landing without being battered to a pulp first by the running sea. One of the islands had been lived on when the Bishop had been built.

I recalled that teams of skin divers were at work off the Gilstone Ledge diving for treasure from the *Association*, the flagship of Admiral Sir Cloudesley Shovell, wrecked with his whole fleet nearly three hundred years ago. It was small comfort. The divers packed up at dusk and puttered back to Hugh Town in their base ship, an inshore sweeper.

The sides of the trough were like black glass now though on the crest the long twilight lingered. I kept going automatically. I seemed to have been doing it for years. Rise and fall, swim across the valley, then up, up again, into the half-light, look frantically around, try desperately to stay for a second or two longer up there in the world of light and air while salt-rimmed eyes strove hopelessly for a glimpse of a sail, a hull, anything floating that would give me hope, then down again into the abyss. That was where I would finish down there in the dark. Sooner or later I would stay there. On one of the waves I would never make its crest. It would go over me and I could be done for, a cold lump of lifeless flesh rolling in the tide, food for the congers that live round the Bishop.

When I heard it first coming down wind, a long thin screeching sound, I ignored it for a trick of the senses due to weakness and exposure; the beginning of the end. Then I heard it again, and recognised it for what it was, my name being called over the wind, long and drawn out. "M-a-r-t-i-n!" It came again while I fought my way to the next crest with hope flooding into me giving me life like a transfusion.

"Here!" I bawled, treadmilling with my feet, while I cupped both hands round my salt-laden mouth. "Over here!"

I kept yelling, even while I was in the trough, finding the breath and the strength to use it from God knows where.

Then I saw her, a small sailing dinghy, cutter-rigged, with a dark sail which was probably red. Christ! I thought, why had I not seen her before? She swooped into the valley of water, then up again rearing like a shying horse, then over the top out of sight. But I knew where to look for her, and I saw her, coming about, handled by an expert. He'd seen me and I knew his plan; bring her up to me then luff so that I could get aboard over the stern.

It was Meg and sailing the yacht alone. She handled the small craft beautifully in that rearing sea, letting tiller and mainsail go at precisely the right moment so that the craft fetched up head to wind bucking over the long swell but giving me the chance to get my hands over the counter and hang on.

She pulled me aboard somehow, bent over me for a moment while I sprawled on the boards like a spent mackerel.

"Oh, Martin! It's a miracle. Thank God I've found you," was all she had time to say before she got back to sailing.

"Towel and jerseys," she shouted from the tiller, "in the locker. This is Jim Benton's cutter. She's a beauty!"

"So are you, Meg," I said silently, not having

the strength to mouth the words. Bare wet boards had never felt so good to my trembling hands.

I managed to jam myself to windward while I towelled my torso with lifeless arms. The air was warmer than the sea, and as soon as I had a couple of thick navy jerseys on I felt the warmth seeping back into my tired bones.

Meg was occupied with her sailing. There was still enough light for her to see the burgee at the mast head, and she was bearing away north-east. The wind was a point or two south of west, not dead aft, but near enough to make it tricky sailing with the swell chasing us. She was aiming to run east of St. Agnes to bear north-west into St. Mary's Sound and round Garrison into harbour.

I waited till we had St. Agnes on our port beam, snoring along in a lessening sea before I asked questions.

"What happened, Meg? Mine is a simple tale of failure. They knocked me out, stowed me in the forepeak having stripped the pants off me, and threw me overboard as soon as they were clear of the Western Isles. Felix was not on board."

"I know. He's at home. It was a trick,

Martin. I waited on the beach for about ten minutes after you'd gone aboard and finally rushed off to find the Reeves-Galways and Chester in the town if I could. I must have just missed them going back to the house. So I phoned, and Steve came down in the car to pick me up. Reeves-Galway was livid with rage. The man's inhuman, I think. I'm sure he didn't care twopence for what had happened to the boy. He was just furious that it should have ever have happened at all, and it was mostly directed against you and me, I can tell you."

"No need to tell me, Meg. I'd guessed it."

She tightened the mainsheet some as the tiller went over to take us northwards clear of St. Agnes.

"Well," she resumed in her clear voice, "I was on the point of blowing my own top because of his lack of concern for the boy, when the doorbell rang. Guess who, Martin. It was Mr. and Mrs. Cookson with little Felix holding hands between them! It's a fact. Their story was that they had been out for their afternoon stroll beyond Old Town then they met the boy running along the path blubbering his eyes out. He told them that some men had bundled him into a car behind the beach, taken him some way, then let him go. He was lost, of course. Recognising him as belonging to Reeves-Galway the Cooksons had simply brought him home. Cookson produced a note which he said had been pinned to the boy's pants. It read: 'Let this be a warning. See how easy it is.' Something like that."

"And Reeves-Galway swallowed it, of course?"

"Hook, line and sinker," Meg laughed. "Drinks for the rescuers, polite chit-chat in the lounge. What a creep that Cookson is! In the meantime I was biting my nails worrying about you aboard the *Jezebel*. When the Cooksons had departed . . . Chester was ordered to drive them back to their hotel . . . I tackled Reeves-Galway and he laughed, Martin. Said that he'd just learnt that you'd got the job under false pretences, and that as far as he was concerned you could rot in hell. I ran out and met Steve coming back from Delgardens. He ran me down to the harbour. The *Jezebel* was still there, so I decided to watch and wait."

Out in the Sound the sea was livelier as we drew away from the St. Agnes's lee. The Peninnis light flashed steadily to starboard and way ahead we could see lights on Garrison.

Sanctuary was just around the corner. God! But I was tired, weary, hungry and thirsty most of all with the salt left by the sea stinging my mouth and throat.

"Then I began to wonder," Meg went on. "Supposing the *Jezebel* got under way with you aboard? I thought perhaps it would be better if I watched from seaward in a boat in case they left. So I rang Jim Benton and he gave me permission to use his cutter. I've often sailed her alone following the gigs when they're racing. Jim rows in the Samson gig. She's still called *Samson* but she's crewed from all over. A couple of visitors helped me get the cutter into the water, and I began cruising around outside the harbour. Sure enough the *Jezebel* showed signs of life round about nine. One of them took the *Dolphin*'s dinghy and beached it. Another followed in their own and brought him back. Then they slipped the mooring and the *Jezebel* jogged out of harbour."

Meg paused. I could just see her at the tiller, her short buttery hair whipped this way and that by the wind. Her orange-coloured life-jacket still carried a faint air of luminosity in the darkness. I guessed that she must be tired as I was.

I've always been attracted to people of action, probably because I consider myself one. My heart went out to Meg, not so much in gratitude just then, but in admiration. I thought of some of the so-called sophisticated dames I had knocked around with when the kitty had been full, and my mouth twisted in disgust. This island girl was one in a million.

"At first," Meg continued, "I guessed their destination as St. Agnes. I could follow them easily with the wind on my beam. They were going at half speed and there wasn't much chance of them increasing it with the sea that was running. But I daren't get too close. I began to worry when they headed into Smith Sound and bore off southwards with the Western Isles a cable's length to starboard. The sea was really awkward, and I was having a job to keep them in sight what with the *Jezebel* losing herself at times in the swell, and the cutter too. Fortunately I saw them coming back."

Her voice faltered. "Martin it was a most dreadful decision I had to make. I couldn't decide whether to go about and follow, or go on. I couldn't think why they'd made the trip at all unless it was to ditch you, but I just couldn't believe they'd do such a thing. In the end I calculated that they'd been about half a mile ahead, did a rapid sum involving speed, time, and directions of turn, then when I'd reached the pre-calculated spot . . . I hoped I was to windward of it, I began shouting your name. Then I saw you on the crest of the wave. It was a miracle."

"Maybe," I said, "but it was also sheer guts and determination on your part, Meg, and I'm eternally grateful to you. There could be a penalty for saving my life. You realise that?"

"What's that?" she asked, laughing.

"You'll find out," I grinned.

Garrison came up on the starboard bow. Meg, careless of a lee shore so close to home, skimmed past Steval and Rat Island, then we were in under the friendly light on the pier head. We dropped the mainsail, and Meg threaded her way through the darkened yachts powered by the jib till the keel grated close to the beach.

Tired as we were it was going to be one hell of a job to get the cutter high and dry on the sand, but neither us even so much as thought of doing anything else.

We were wrestling with her at the bows when a dark figure loomed at the water's edge.

"Is that you, Meg? Martin?"

It was Steve Chester. He took off his shoes and socks and splashed alongside.

"Jumping Jesus!" he exclaimed. "I'd given you till midnight. Then I was going to call out the police, the Coastguards, and the ruddy lifeboat. What happened?"

"Tell you," I grunted. "Let's get the cutter ashore first."

We hauled her, with his fresh strength to help, above the tide mark and then squatting on the sand, with the cigarette he gave me soothing my nerve ends, I told him what had happened.

He didn't waste time on exclamations.

"What are you going to do about it, Martin? You can't let 'em get away with that."

"Cookson!" I said. "Cookson is paying them. They admitted as much. I'm going to get that fat slob into a corner and I'm going to sink my fingers into his neck till he squeals for mercy, and tells me what it's all about. That's what I'm going to do."

I felt Meg's hand on my arm.

172

"No, Martin. You'll only bring yourself down to his level if you do."

"Maybe, Meg, but with types like Cookson you can't reach 'em till you get down to their level."

"Martin," Chester put in, "you ain't going to like this. You're sacked. He's slung you out. He stood over me while I packed your stuff. I've got your cases in the car now. He said he didn't give a damn what I did with them so long as I took them out of his house."

"It figures," I said. "Cookson put in the word. What the hell goes between those two? I'll find out."

"It would be more practical," Meg suggested, "if you considered your own position. Where are you going to sleep tonight? You won't find accommodation easily at this hour in the middle of the season."

"I'll doss down on the *Dolphin*," I answered. "Or is Reeves-Galway going grave-searching again tonight?"

"I wouldn't be surprised," Chester growled. "Maybe he's bawling for me right now. I've been prowling up and down the beach for a couple of hours. They told me Meg had gone out single-handed in a cutter. No shipwrecked matelot has looked harder for a sail coming in than me."

"Thank you, Steve," Meg laughed. "I didn't know you cared."

"What are you going to do, Meg?" I asked her. "Going to carry on?"

There was a pause.

"I must Martin. I need the money. Flower-growing in the Scillies is a dying industry."

She was referring to her parents who kept a small flower farm. Competition in the form of air freight from the Channel Islands is too much for the Scillonians compelled to use the steamer and rail to the London market.

"Besides," she went on, "there's young Felix. I'm beginning to like the boy. He needs me. I can do a lot for him in three months."

She scrambled to her feet.

"Come on, Martin. I've thought of something. If Steve has the car he can run us over to Pelistry. You can have my bed at home. The folks won't mind."

They were in bed themselves when we arrived at the small greystone cottage above the bay, and a little put out till Meg told them I was Uncle Horace's nephew then they couldn't do enough for me. The old lady insisted on

174

cooking me a gigantic meal of bacon and eggs when she heard that I'd been in the sea. She also brewed tea whilst the meal was frying, and I swallowed three cups straight off. It tasted like nectar.

Chester, though he didn't say so, was anxious about getting back to Coronel House. Reeves-Galway would be raging if he'd planned to cross to Samson again.

"Don't tell him you found me," I instructed Meg. "It might be a pleasant surprise for him one day, and I certainly don't want Cookson to know."

Chester had unloaded my cases, and when I had seen them off, I hauled the cases upstairs to Meg's little room under the sloping roof. It smelt of her. Jasmine, I thought it was.

Her bed was soft. I slept like a dead man at a lantern lecture. Her folks were up early, but left me sleeping till eight. After breakfast I went out to the lane and managed to cadge a lift in a farm van to Hugh Town.

It was nine fifteen when I arrived outside Delgardens at the bottom of Garrison Hill. Cookson, I was sure, would be finishing his breakfast. I could see him in my mind's eye playing the gentleman, remembering to use his napkin, pulling out Julia's chair for her when they got up from table. Cookson was in for one hell of a nasty surprise. I would stalk the bastard, with the patience of a hunting cat, till I caught him on his own and then I would pounce.

But it was I who received the surprise. I lost patience eventually lurking by the hotel's garden wall in the bright morning sunshine. I went in to the reception desk and asked for him.

"I'm sorry," the girl said. "Mr. and Mrs. Cookson have left the island. They were booked out on the eight o'clock helicopter this morning."

10

I LEFT the Scillies two days later. I had no trouble in keeping in touch with Meg and Chester, because they came seeking me. Then Reeves-Galway decided to go cruising on the *Dolphin*. He told them that he wanted to take advantage of the continuing fine weather, but he had kept up his grave-searching on Samson and Chester reckoned that the yawl would finish up off the island every night. Daylight searching was out because Samson was popular with visitors during the day, and the launches from St. Mary's landed a quota of them every morning, picking them up again in the afternoon.

Meg was unhappy at the prospect. I did my best to dissuade her from going but she couldn't do that without turning in the job and she needed the money. I had to sympathise with her there. It was the main reason why I decided to go home, where I was used to ekeing out a poverty stricken existence. I couldn't impose on her parents any longer and I was unable to find accommodation on the island whose visitors already outnumbered the residents.

Before I left I called in the Post Office for any message from Everard, but all he had sent me was a description of Albert Blagdon which was entirely redundant after Sergeant Bolt's efforts. I considered telephoning Everard, tried twice and was told each time that he was out of town. Nor would his department tell me where.

The *Jezebel* no longer moored in Hugh Town harbour. Chester said that they had crossed to Tresco and were anchored at New Grimsby. Though he and Reeves-Galway had been unmolested on Samson for the further night they had gone searching he was certain that they had not been alone on the island. Perhaps Sprott Bros and Co. had been reluctant to act without the guiding genius of Cookson.

I caught the afternoon boat on the Friday, and trundled the Mini-Cooper into the garage at 1 a.m. on the Saturday. I was up again at eight. I knew where Cookson lived. At least I had a fair idea. When I had first joined the Belsize Agency, and we'd chatted, he had talked airily of his twenty-thousand-pound home in the country near East Grinstead. That was enough for me. I was down there within ninety minutes, parked, and searching the local telephone directory. He was in it. John B. Cookson (the B stood for Belsize), The Coopers, Half Foot Lane.

A van driver told me that Half Foot Lane was about three miles along the Tunbridge Wells Road. It matched with the Dormansland telephone number.

The weather was continuing fine in England as well as in the Scillies and the countryside was bursting with early summer life.

Half Foot Lane meandered through woodland powdered with bluebells. It was not much wider than a cart track but its surface was good macadam. The town was reaching out into the country, and the lane fed some very comfortable discreetly sheltered homes. The Coopers was one of these; a big ranch-style bungalow squatting in about half an acre of lawn behind a screen of trees.

I discovered this after I had parked the Mini on a convenient verge farther up the lane and walked back. The drive in displayed the name painted on a highly polished slice of tree-trunk stuck on a post inside the gates.

I took to the trees once I was inside, and reccied the place from cover. The bungalow had a double garage, the doors of which were open, displaying the rear end of Cookson's Jaguar and what must have been Gloria's Mini. Both were red. I could see no signs of life within the house.

I waited. I had all day. Cookson was a five-day week man, as a rule, and the presence of the two cars suggested that he and Gloria were at home. Bird life was noisy around me including the blatant call of a cuckoo every now and again.

Then Cookson appeared round the side of the bungalow. As usual he was as elegant as all Savile Row, even in casual wear. He went into the garage, started up the Mini, backed out and moved the car as far as the front door, where he left it to go indoors. Presently Gloria appeared pulling on her gloves. She stowed her curves into the Mini, and drove off, turning out of the drive in the direction of the town.

I gave her five minutes, then moved cautiously round the perimeter of the property till I was able to view the rear of the bungalow and its kitchen door which was standing ajar. It was possible that the Cooksons employed a servant. If they did then I wanted to know it before I made my call. But the place remained as quiet and as remote as a sanctuary with only the birds showing life. A big woodpecker ran across the lawn. It was green with a red crest, a beautiful bird. I watched it exploring the grass for a minute or two, then it flew off giving out its peculiar laughing cry. A black cat, stiff-legged with frustration stalked on to the lawn.

I crossed the grass from my cover, tiptoed over the flagged terrace and went into the kitchen. It was all white and duck-egg blue with rows of glass-fronted cupboards and a tiled floor of the same colours shining like a mirror.

I opened a door which I found to be at the back of a wide carpeted hall. It was quiet save for a tall modern clock of grandfatherly proportions that ticked ponderously. Where the hell was Cookson?

I counted two doors on my right and one on my left, but the hall was T shaped. When I crept forward to explore the recesses I smelt cigarette smoke. The door at the end of the right-hand recess was open and when I had moved cautiously up to it I knew Cookson was in the room. I could hear the rustle of papers and the smell of smoke was stronger.

The door when I pushed it gently inwards seemed inordinately stout and heavy. The jamb had sockets for bolts in it, top, bottom and middle.

Cookson was kneeling at the opened door of a safe. His broad back entirely blocked my view of the safe's interior.

I expect he called the room a study but it was in fact little more than an office, with a desk, a telephone, a glass-fronted bookcase, and the safe. The two windows were heavily barred on the outside.

"Get up, Cookson!" I rasped.

The sound of my voice was the first intimation he had of my presence. His head screwed round as quick as a startled hen's. Even when he saw me he still didn't believe me. It was not until he was on his feet that it came home to him. His face went green and seemed to fold inwards, leaving it a blubbery mask of fear and tension.

"Get a grip on yourself," I warned him. "You're no good to me flaked out. I want you alive and fully conscious, Cookie . . . old boy," I added in a parody of his own style of address.

He moved for the desk, and considering his seventeen stone he moved damned fast, but I was expecting him. I dropped on my hands and my two feet slammed into him high above his fat hip. They knocked him into the wall between the windows. He went scrabbling along the carpet on all fours, but by that time I was on my feet between him and the desk. The flat of my right foot smacked into his face, and he bowed over sideways with his hands to his injured mug.

"Don't!" he screamed in his high-pitched voice as shrill as a woman's. "Don't!"

He wanted to shrink his bulk into a ball on the carpet, drawing his knees up to his chin and covering his head with his hands. He seemed to dwindle before my eyes like a slug with salt on its tail.

I kept one eye on him whilst with the other I explored the drawers in the desk. The top right-hand one revealed an opened box in which was a Lüger-type automatic, complete with a spare clip loaded, and a small wire brush for cleaning. I put the gun and its spare clip in my pocket.

"Get up!" I snarled at the grovelling Cookson. Contempt amounting to nausea was welling in my throat. I had intended beating him up so that he would remember the commission he had given the Sprott brothers to drown me at sea for the rest of his days. Now, seeing him in a fat ball at my feet, expecting the boot to go in, I couldn't bring myself to start. Meg had been right. I could not get myself low enough for Cookson. Besides, the opened safe had given me ideas. This room with its barred windows and electrically operated bolts on its doors was obviously the spot where Cookson kept his crooked secrets. Maybe I could help myself to a few, spread them around in the right places and the law would catch up with Cookson. Prison would hurt him more than any beating up though it might be slower in action.

I stirred his fat hide with my toe.

"On your feet, Cookie!"

I dragged out his desk chair and spun it towards him as he peered up unbelievingly.

He got to his feet at last. I lifted one of mine and pushed him into the chair.

"Sorry to use my feet so much," I said, "but I can't bring myself to using my hands when dealing with snakes. But don't let it tempt you into doing something rash, Cookie, old boy. I have your gun in my pocket."

"What . . . what do you want, Martin?" he piped. "Look, I know I got Reeves-Galway to sack you, but I'll make up the money. With a bonus . . ."

"That's an idea." I glanced at the safe. It was stuffed with notes. I could see bundles of them on a shelf along with boxes and round metal cans. "Perhaps I'll help myself, Cookie. I want information, and don't bother to lie. The Sprott brothers along with their two helpers were obliging enough to admit that you were paying them before they chucked me into the Atlantic. What goes between you and Reeves-Galway? Give me the history of it. When did you first meet him?"

His little dark eyes flickered with hope and cunning. I could read his mind. It was saying, "I can fool this big Marine any day. What the hell have I been worrying about?"

Aloud he said:

"Reeves-Galway employed the agency years ago when he divorced his first wife. That's when I met him."

"Move on to last year. You were staying in the Scillies at the same time as Reeves-Galway. He was employing Blagdon on his yacht at times. Blagdon worked for you at one time. Did you make the introduction?"

"Well . . . yes . . . I suppose I did, old boy,"

185

he answered with a return to his usual public-school role.

"That means you did," I nodded. "Go on. Move on to April this year, when you were staying at Delgardens in company with Reeves-Galway and a certain Colonel Sikes. What happened then?"

"So I was right," he squeaked excitedly. "I guessed that you wanted the job with Reeves-Galway because of Sikes. He was a Marine . . ."

"Don't get bold, Cookie," I warned him. "*Please!* Don't get brave. Just answer the question, eh?"

His nose, with an odd delayed action, had started to bleed. It dripped steadily on to his cream silk shirt making ugly dark red blotches. He noticed it, drew the back of his hand across his face and stared horrified at the blood on it.

"Oh, God!" he croaked. He started to get out of the chair and my foot sent him rocketing back.

"I was only going to fetch a handkerchief," he wailed.

"Don't bother. You've got plenty of blood. Buckets of it. You won't miss a few drops. Tell me what happened in April. You weren't there by happy coincidence, Cookie. You were there by design."

He was staring at me now with hate and venom in his eyes.

"You must know why I was there. Reeves-Galway told you that Sikes was smuggling diamonds, didn't he? Before you went grave-searching? I knew it was going on. I heard it from other sources. Okay! I keep my ears open for the chance of making money. I know the Scillies well, so I hired some help with a boat and went over there. I didn't know Reeves-Galway was going to be there, or that Delgardens would be open."

"How did Reeves-Galway know that Sikes was smuggling diamonds?"

"Sikes sold him a couple of big stones. They were rough. Reeves-Galway had them made up into a couple of drop ear-rings for Lola."

"Go on. What happened the night Sikes disappeared off his yacht?"

Cookson spread out his fat hands.

"Your guess is as good as mine, Martin," he smirked. "I don't know what happened to Sikes."

I slipped off the corner of the desk where I

had perched, and stood over him menacingly. He flinched.

"Then what the hell is all this malarkey on Samson about? Don't lie to me, Cookie. Both you and Reeves-Galway believe him to be buried on the island."

"That's what Reeves-Galway told you," he piped. "He's not looking for a grave, and nor are my blokes. Sikes cached a load of diamonds on the island that night. He fooled the lot of us. He sailed off towards St. Martin's. I'd been keeping a careful eye on his comings and goings and as soon as he left harbour I phoned my blokes, who were on Tresco. Didn't want to rouse any suspicions by keeping them in harbour at St. Mary's . . ."

"They were using the *Jezebel*?"

"Not in April. Something heavier and faster. I forget its name. Cost me a packet to charter, I can tell you. Hundreds, Martin!"

He could not resist the mention of money. He assumed that the whole wide world worshipped the stuff the same as he. Maybe he was not far wrong.

"And they were anchored off New Grimsby?" I asked.

"That's right. One of them was staying in the

pub so that I could contact them at any time after dark, when Sikes was likely to go. The bastard was probably drunk, and they were late getting away. They couldn't find Sikes. He must have veered off west between St. Martin's and Tresco till he was clear out in the Atlantic, taking a line on the Bishop light, made his rendezvous, picked up his load, and sailed for Samson. My blokes were making for home when they saw him leaving the beach in his dinghy. It was a brilliant moonlit night."

"What the devil was he doing on Samson?"

"I told you. He cached his haul, buried it or whatever."

"How do you know that?"

Cookson stirred his fat restlessly. His nose had stopped its bleeding and he seemed to have forgotten it. There was some colour in his face now, but his little black eyes were as malicious as ever.

"Look, Martin, I didn't hire those blokes to murder Sikes, and I didn't ask questions. I don't know exactly what happened. They boarded him, knocked him out, searched the yacht and him. No diamonds."

Cookson paused. He licked his lips.

"This is surmise. I didn't want to know . . ."

"Out of sight. Out of mind," I jeered. "You grieve me, Cookie. You were just as responsible as if you'd been there handing Sikes the *coup-de-grâce*. But you'll pay, old boy. I'll see to that."

"They didn't mean to kill him," he wailed. "For Crissakes, Martin. They weren't exactly skilled assassins. Sikes was a tricky number. When he came round they started questioning him. He admitted that he'd hidden the haul on Samson. He had the idea that the Customs might be on to him. Then he fooled 'em somehow and started the fight. He threw a couple of them overboard, and the—well, you know how it is—one of them hit him too hard. He was excited, and . . . Sikes was dead. You can guess the rest. They took his body, and towed his yacht to deep water clear of the Islands, dumped him overboard and let the cutter drift. Satisfied?"

"Not quite. Why the hell should Reeves-Galway bother about a cache of diamonds? He's a rich man."

"You'd better ask him," he retorted. "I don't know. Diamonds fascinate some people, paupers or millionaires."

Had he been telling the truth? The story was

190

plausible enough, if I could believe that Sikes had actually been smuggling diamonds, but there was a flaw in it. He realised that I was distrusting him.

"That's God's truth, Martin, as far as I know it," he squeaked eagerly.

"But you showed no interest in Samson till Reeves-Galway arrived, and started searching," I pointed out. "You ask me to believe that you were aware of a fortune in diamonds buried on Samson and did nothing till there was a risk of Reeves-Galway finding them? I'm not that simple."

"Be your age, Martin," he croaked. "My blokes were combing the island a week after Sikes disappeared. They found nothing. Reeves-Galway might have had better luck. That's why they followed him."

Still it didn't ring true. The men from the *Jezebel* had made it plain that they'd wanted Samson left alone. They'd not acted as if they'd been waiting for Reeves-Galway to dig up the haul so that they could hi-jack it. But they had waited till daylight before they had actually attacked.

Cookson got up carefully from his chair as if he expected that at any moment my boot would put him back in it. When he found that he had been allowed to gain his feet he ducked suddenly towards the safe, put in a hand and pulled out a packet of money.

"Here, Martin," he exhorted scrambling to his feet again and thrusting the bundle at me, "a hundred fivers. You have these, eh? No hard feelings. I owe you that much old boy."

"Thanks," I said, taking the packet.

He began closing the safe door.

"Put it back, Cookie."

He wouldn't take it and I threw the packet into the safe. The door was nearly closed when I hauled him off it, and stooping pulled out a big sealed envelope and three round tins. They were tapes.

"No!" he screamed, pulling at my arm. "Not those. They're no use to you. Put them back, Martin. Please!"

For answer I dug him in the stomach with my elbow. He broke away. I paused to eye the remainder of the safe's contents and it was not a wise move. When I turned he was coming at me with the big office chair high over his head to smash down on me. His face was yellow with rage and contorted with hate; his black eyes snapping.

I slipped to one side and he smashed the chair to pieces on the steel top of the safe. The desk was next to me and I dumped the tapes and envelope on it as he came at me like a maniac, screaming filth and clawing at my face.

I hit him four times before he went down. He wasn't out, just dead scared of taking more. He had so much blubber on him a really damaging blow was difficult to land.

I picked up the envelope and tins, walked round him, and left him there sobbing with rage and frustration into his own carpet.

11

IT was Saturday, and the banks had shut by the time I was back in Kensington. I was not particularly anxious to keep Cookson's property in the flat over the week-end. The ferocity with which he had attacked me after I had helped myself from the safe was proof enough of its importance to him. Whilst I was sure that he would not make an effort to recover it in person I was equally sure that he could get into touch with a number of tough gentlemen by telephone who would be only too pleased to take on the job of recovery, and to beat the living daylights out of me in the process. I wanted Everard to have the tapes and the envelope, which by the feel of it contained photographs. I could have delivered them to the nearest police station but my mind jibbed at the lengthy explanations I would have to make.

I rang Everard's office and the call was taken by a duty officer, who was a cagey number. When I told him that all I wanted was to leave a small travel bag to wait Major Everard's return he wouldn't play unless I told him exactly what was in the bag.

Further questions followed when I said: "An envelope and three tins of tape." I told him: "Forget it. I'll keep 'em myself till Everard gets back." He was right, of course. Any lunatic could leave a bag with a bomb in it. I took the bag along to Charing Cross station and lodged it in the left-luggage office.

It never occurred to me to examine the photographs. I could guess at their nature. Blown-up prints from the negatives of shots taken by his operatives' buttonhole cameras; the spicey ones; those he could use for blackmail when the time was ripe. The same with the tapes. I didn't possess a recorder, and I was certainly not going to buy one out of my slender resources in order to hear conversations between Cookson and his clients. He probably recorded everything that was said in his office, and transferred the promising material on to edited tapes.

I spent the week-end at the club. I fully expected my flat to have been burgled but when I went round there on Monday morning everything was ship-shape. I wondered if Cookson had given up the ghost, or had realised that I would put his property in a spot virtually impossible for him to raid, and was waiting his time. He would have to hurry.

Everard returned on Wednesday and wanted to see me when I telephoned. I had heard nothing from the Scillies, an omission that nagged at my mind because both Meg and Chester had promised to write. But if they were living on the *Dolphin* access to a post office would not have been easy, and was probably subject to Reeves-Galway's whim.

I retrieved the bag from the left luggage at Charing Cross and took a taxi to Queen's Gate.

Everard looked fit and tanned. He raised his eyebrows when I dumped the bag on his desk but said nothing other than to tell me to sit down, which I did. He pushed the cigarette box in my direction.

"You must be classed as a civil servant for holidays," I suggested. "How long do you get, eight weeks?"

"Six," he smiled. "What's been happening, Martin? I thought you were in the Scillies."

"I was fired," I said, helping myself to a cigarette. "Let me tell you how."

He listened without comment.

"All I wanted to do," I concluded, "was to catch up with Cookson. I caught him last

Saturday morning in his own home. He talked. Sikes was smuggling diamonds, and hid the haul on Samson because he thought the Customs on St. Mary's were suspicious and might give him a going over, I suppose. Cookson's men saw him leaving the island. They nobbled him . . ."

I gave him the rest of it. Then I opened the bag and brought out the envelope and the tapes.

"I haven't looked at the photographs, or played the tapes. I leave that to you. I'm sure you can find material enough to give you a line on Cookson's blackmailing tricks, and put him away for years."

Everard nodded.

"If we can trace a victim who is willing to give evidence," he put in as a rider. "Do you think that is the truth of what happened to Raymond Sikes?"

I put a match to my cigarette and smoked thoughtfully for a few seconds.

"Probably not," I said at last, "because I wouldn't trust Cookson farther than I could carry an elephant. But I think it's somewhere near the truth, Charles. There is a flaw in Cookson's story. His blokes were not waiting for Reeves-Galway to find Sikes's diamonds the night we went grave-searching. They didn't want us on the island at all which is not the same thing."

Everard stirred in his chair.

"Ray Sikes was *not* a smuggler, Martin," he declared emphatically. "Get that into your head. Which disposes of Cookson's story as one long lie. Besides, even if it were near the truth, there is one bigger flaw in it than you mentioned. How does Reeves-Galway know that the diamonds were cached on Samson? You surely don't suppose that Cookson told him?"

"No," I said weakly. "I should have thought of that. But Reeves-Galway was out himself in the *Dolphin* that night. Could he have perhaps seen Sikes go ashore on Samson?"

Everard took a folder out of his desk and opened it.

"And guessed what he was up to?" he asked without looking up. "Forget it, Martin. Diamond-smuggling is out." He paused with a finger on the file and smiled. "Superintendent Trevillian has been good enough to send me copies of the reports on the case made by his detective sergeant . . ."

"Bolt," I supplied. "I met him. An odd

character. He made one cryptic remark I want to ask you about . . ."

"Later, Martin. Bolt's enquiries were routine but thorough. For instance he compiled a history of the movements of all shipping in the neighbourhood of the Scillies on the night of the 28th April, including those of all yachts and launches in and out of the island harbours; not only St. Mary's, but Tresco, St. Martin's and St. Agnes."

Everard referred to the file again.

"Here is an item that disposes of Cookson's story once and for all. There was no strange motor craft at New Grimsby that night. But . . . this is odd, Martin . . . one turned up a week later. According to the locals it moved over to Samson the same night. The party on it were thought to have landed. Lights were seen, and flashes suggesting that photographs were being taken."

"That would be when Cookson claimed to have been treasure hunting," I pointed out.

Everard raised his eyebrows.

"Coincidence, d'you think? The craft need not have been connected with Cookson in any way at all. Tell me, Martin. What did you think of Reeves-Galway?"

"Not much," I said. "In fact I hated his guts. The feeling was mutual, I think. He hated mine. The man's had so much money all his life he's got a touch of megalomania. Understandable, perhaps. On the other hand he hates publicity, and maybe that doesn't go with megalomania. Perhaps he should welcome the limelight. I just don't know, Charles. I'm not clever enough. Anyway, he's a very unstable character at heart, and I'm sure too much money is no good to a man like that. He drinks a lot. He has a smiling exterior which changes to one of snarling ferocity if he is put out in any way. When he becomes excited he shows more than a little hysteria. After we had been attacked on Samson, and had beaten them off, Reeves-Galway wanted to charge after them. He had a knife, the only weapon available. Chester and I had to hold him down. Mind you, he'd taken a knock on the head, which may have been responsible."

"Perhaps," Everard remarked cryptically. "Perhaps not. I've been busy on Reeves-Galway, probing into his history, because it seems to me, or it did as soon as I received Trevillian's report, that he has been in the

200

centre of the odd happenings in the Scillies starting with Blagdon. Sergeant Bolt . . ."

"Traced Blagdon to Tresco," I put in. "He told me."

"And reports that a man answering Blagdon's description was employed at intervals on Reeves-Galway's yacht. It's unfortunate in a way that the Cornish CID when it was established that Blagdon had gone to Penzance failed to trace him to Tresco at the time . . ."

"He changed his name, Charles, and did the discovery of a corpse that might or might not have been Blagdon's, the subject I assume of nothing but a general enquiry, warrant a really close investigation?"

"A matter of opinion," Everard said. "I don't suppose it mattered since Reeves-Galway has denied employing him, and certainly there is no witness to say that he actually *sailed* on the *Dolphin* with Blagdon as a crewman."

"Which, if it came to the point, would be the only sort of a witness of any value to a court of law," I suggested. "Sergeant Bolt, however, faced with the investigation of a second mysterious happening in the Scillies, or with what might have been the second if Blagdon had been in the Scillies, wondered if there was any connection and had another go at tracing Blagdon. Shrewd Sergeant Bolt."

"Shrewd indeed," Everard observed. "A man after my own heart. He made the routine enquiries in Delgardens after Sikes had disappeared. He not only asked each guest what he knew of Sikes, but he also asked them what they knew of the other guests."

He helped himself to a cigarette in an absent-minded way.

"You'll recall that I told you there was a churchman amongst the guests?" he went on, and when I nodded, "Archdeacon Tibbs, who when questioned said that although he did not know Reeves-Galway, other than as a fellow guest in the hotel, he had actually seen him before in a place called L'Hôpital de Grise, near Geneva . . ."

"Ah," I said, "I wondered if you'd mention that. It was Sergeant Bolt's cryptic remark."

Everard took advantage of my interruption to light his cigarette.

"I'll go on," he said. "Archdeacon Tibbs also volunteered the information that when he had mentioned it to Reeves-Galway the millionaire rather rudely implied that Tibbs was talking through his shovel hat. He'd never been near the place. Tibbs was annoyed, which was probably why he mentioned the incident to Sergeant Bolt in the first place."

"And the sergeant evidently saw some significance in Reeves-Galway denying that he'd been there. Why? It's a hospital . . ."

"Of a sort," Everard agreed. "It is in fact a very exclusive and very expensive private institution of a kind that no longer exists in this country. To put it in the vernacular, Martin, it's a private looney-bin or nut-house."

I whistled, then a point occurred to me.

"But if the Archdeacon had been a patient there can you rely upon him having told the truth about Reeves-Galway?"

"I think so," Everard smiled. "The hospital is situated reasonably close to the Geneva Lausanne highway, not far from Nyon, and the Canton authorities prevailed upon the owners to set up a small accident unit. That's why the Archdeacon was there. He was recovering from shock after a car crash, sunning his clerical bones in the extensive grounds when he saw Reeves-Galway, or claims that he did."

"And did he, Charles? You've checked?"

"In person, Martin. That's where I have been this past week. Enquiries by telex were negative. If Reeves-Galway had been a patient then it was under another name."

"Is that possible?"

"For you or me probably not, but for a man with Reeves-Galway's money, entirely possible. I went out there with his description but with no photograph."

He paused and sighed.

"It was bloody hard going, Martin. I'd envisaged a quick flip to Cointrin airport, a taxi to the hospital to make my enquiries, then back to the airport. But the citadels of the very rich are well guarded. They refused point blank to give me any information regarding a patient. I was not there in an official capacity, but as a private individual. There was not enough evidence of crime committed to warrant an official visit, and if there had been it would have been the job of the Cornish CID, certainly not of my department in the Metropolitan Police."

"What did you do?" I asked.

"I had the choice of two alternatives. Either to make it official which would have meant lengthy cables of explanation to London and cables back to Geneva for the support of the local police. London would surely have had to contact Penzance. It would have taken too much time. The only cash I had was my basic travel allowance of fifty pounds, and Switzerland after devaluation is hideously expensive."

"The alternative?"

"To contact the only Swiss National I knew, a banker in Zürich and an influential man, to enlist his aid. I telephoned him and he promised to pull a few strings. But it took time. After two days he came through with an introduction to the Chief of Police in Geneva, a man named Alphonse Marechal, who is of French origin."

Everard paused. He stubbed out his cigarette, which was only half smoked.

"Even then it was not plain sailing. Marechal came out to the hospital with me, and to give them their due once his presence had made it official, they couldn't do enough for me. The trouble was that Reeves-Galway had stayed there not only under another name but an assumed nationality. All I had was a physical description and the knowledge that he had been there during the spring of the year before last."

"The year before he appeared in the Scillies and employed Blagdon," I said, getting it right in my mind.

"That's it," Everard went on. "Searching the records was useless. The hospital is a pretty big

205

place, housed in what used to be a nobleman's mansion to which three wings have been added from time to time. They can cater for over a hundred patients, classified into various groups according to their peculiar mental disabilities and each group with its own doctors and medical staff, who change fairly frequently. My only hope was that some medical orderly or servant would remember Reeves-Galway. It might not have been so bad if only I had known *why* he had gone there; if he had been a schizophrenic or a dipso who, I might add, form a large proportion of the clientele."

"So what did they do?" I asked. "Parade all the attendants in a long line for you?"

Everard grinned.

"Business could not have been all that brisk," he said. "They gave me a room in the hospital and *carte blanche* to wander around questioning the staff, which I did. Fortunately most of them speak English, and my mixture of French and German is not too bad. It was really quite a good spot in which to spend a couple of days," he went on reminiscently. "The estate overlooks the vineyards sloping down to the lake with the French mountains in the distance beyond the water. Very nice, rather wasted on the majority

206

of the patients some of whom were as dotty as March hares, and others whose sole concern was to find out if I had a flask in my hip pocket."

Idly he drew Cookson's envelope across the desk towards him, slit the flap with a finger and pulled out some prints.

"Come on, Charles," I urged. "What happened? Had Reeves-Galway been a patient there?"

"He had indeed, under the name of Victor Ginsburg, a citizen of Bonn. I found an attendant on my second day who remembered him well. He'd been his room orderly. The records showed that Victor Ginsburg was a paranoiac. He had acute depression."

"Is that any help?" I asked. "Surely it's a general term for mental derangement including delusions of grandeur? I could have told them that after two days in his company."

"It was fairly serious, Martin. They wanted him to have leucotomy; that's incision of the frontal lobes of the brain . . ."

"Thanks," I said drily. "And did he?"

"He refused and discharged himself after a month."

"Where does that get us, Charles?" I demanded bitterly. "You've spent good money to find out that Reeves-Galway was a month in the nut-house. OK. Where do we go from here? Listen," I added struck by the thought. "Something . . . some incident or other . . . must have persuaded Reeves-Galway to enter himself as a patient in the first place. What was it, Charles? It must have had a grave import to send a man like him voluntarily to the looney-bin."

"Whatever it was the records of the hospital didn't reveal it. Reeves-Galway entered the place without a medical history sheet. The reasons he gave the doctors, who didn't necessarily believe them, was that he suffered intermittently from delusions."

Everard closed the file. "I'm working on it, Martin, but it is not easy. The man has avoided the limelight for years. I'm trying to get a complete history on him from his schooldays . . ."

"Yes, but it's all so vague," I protested. "We've got absolutely nowhere. If Sikes was murdered there must have been a motive. You resolutely refuse to believe that he was a smuggler. That at least would provide a motive . . ."

"I know," he nodded gravely, "but all along I've been impressed by this apparent absolute

lack of motive. Consider the facts, Martin."
Everard put up a hand to pull down a finger on
it as he ticked them off. "The locality is one of
the most law-abiding and peaceful spots on
earth. Sikes was a man of undoubted integrity.
I can't stress that point enough, Martin.
Anything shady or underhand would have been
completely alien to his character. Moreover it
is inconceivable that he could have got mixed
up with anything crooked even by accident in
the Scillies. Do you agree?"

"Cookson was there," I argued, "and not by
accident, nor for a holiday, but for profit."

"That may be but I'm sure that Sikes was
not his target. No, Martin, I've given you the
basic facts. I think we shall find that the reason
for Sikes' death was outside all normal reck-
oning; that it is bizarre and even horrible."

"I've had similar thoughts myself," I
admitted, "but they don't get me anywhere.
For instance if Reeves-Galway's idea that Sikes
was a smuggler and had hidden diamonds on
Samson is so much baloney, and he knows it,
where did the story originate? In his mind, or
Cookson's? Who told whom? And what was he
looking for on Samson, Charles? Because he was
in earnest. Was it actually a grave?"

"Possibly," Everard said mildly. He seemed to have lost interest and had pulled out some prints from Cookson's envelope. He shuffled through them grimacing.

"Not quite pornography," he commented "but close to it. Why on earth do the subjects permit him to take such photographs and to keep them?"

"No option," I said. "Those bold enough to demand the negative don't know how many he's had printed. Something special in that one?"

He was holding one that had been specially enveloped. He slit the flap, and drew out the print. His face changed. Horror and incredulity chased themselves across it.

"My God!" he breathed. "Look at that, Martin."

He passed me the photograph. The subject was a dead man. He was flat on his back in a shallow grave. It was an ugly picture, for the mouth was open and the dead eyes stared at the camera as blank as marbles. No attempt had been made to compose the body. It had been half twisted into its constricted space so that the limbs, already dusted with light soil, were at unnatural angles heightening the indignity of death.

"D'you know who it is, Martin?"

I looked at him and shook my head. Everard was shocked. His eyes were burning and he had gone pale.

"It's Raymond Sikes!" he said.

12

EVERARD put down the telephone over which he had been passing instructions for the immediate detention of John Belsize Cookson.

"I hope they get him," I said, "but if I know Cookie he's a thousand miles away by now. I felt sure he'd make an attempt to recover his property but he didn't. He saw the red light."

I pushed the round tins of tape towards him.

"We ought to play these," I suggested.

The labels on the tins carried a series of numbers obviously a method of indexing the contents, but since we had no possible way of identifying them it meant that we would have to listen to the lot.

Everard took out a reel and examined the tape.

"If this is four track then there is hours of listening ahead of us," he grimaced.

"Very likely," I agreed. "I'm sure he taped every scrap of conversation passed in his office between himself and clients, and he's been in business for years. Those tapes contain the edited stuff."

Everard pressed the switch on his intercom and told his secretary to come in.

"See if you can rustle up a tape recorder," he told her as soon as she appeared. "I'm pretty certain there is one in Commander Rixon's office. Ask him if I can borrow it for twenty-four hours. Perhaps I'd better speak to him myself. Get him on the blower, but tell a messenger to stand by. He can fetch it straightaway."

The blonde gave me a warm smile as she went out. She was a dish. She could have gone skating in her mini-dress and not been inappropriately dressed.

The loan of the recorder was arranged under the old pals' act, and within twenty minutes a messenger had placed it on Everard's desk.

"I hope you've got plenty of time, Martin," Everard said, looking for a plug. "I'm prepared to make it. I hope it won't be wasted."

"I'll bet on that," I declared. "You'll recall that when you first told me about Sikes I hinted that Cookson could have gone to the Scillies well prepared for eavesdropping. I'm sure now that Reeves-Galway was his target. A target for blackmail. Let it roll, Charles."

So we began the audition. My mind could not hope to memorise the long roll-call of voices that poured in procession from the speaker, nor what they were saying. Nearly all of it dealt with divorce. Erring husbands. Erring wives. Shrill voices and deep voices. Through them all Cookson's interjections in his oiliest tones. Some of it was ineffably crude. Much of it was pathetic, and some of it was even funny if you liked that brand of humour. The tapes also contained chosen reports from operatives that were obvious food for blackmail.

Coffee and biscuits came in, but the tapes wound on. We adjourned for lunch at the club and returned in a cab. Everard was giving it priority and told his girl that he would take no telephone calls till we were finished.

An hour later we had reached the second track of the second tape, and I was almost asleep, the inexorable voices from the speaker beginning to wash over me when a voice I recognised jerked me awake. It was Reeves-Galway's and what it had said was:

"Do sit down, Colonel. What will you have to drink?"

"Thanks. Whisky please. Er . . . water. Half and half."

A pause, and I glanced excitedly at Everard.

"Sikes!" he snapped, and leant forward to adjust the volume. This had evidently been transmitted over a radio bug. It was fainter and there was mush in the background.

There was no sequence to the opening conversation. No toast following the pouring of drinks. Cookson must have left the opening passages in the edited version as a means of identification. Reeves-Galway's voice came on again. It had the odd vibrant quality which meant that he was excited. His eyes I knew would be glittering and febrile.

"You don't think that is possible?" he was asking.

"On the contrary. Of course it is possible." Sikes sounded faintly bored and a trifle terse as if he had been irritated by the conversation. "I merely pointed out that the odds would be heavily against you. I'm a trained soldier, practised in moving silently at night. I ought to be able to outrun you and outwit you. I don't say I can but that I ought to be able to do so."

"Why not put it to the test?"

Sikes laughed.

"Really, the argument if you can call it that, has gone far enough. I don't doubt your physical prowess for one moment, Victor. It doesn't bother me. Let's leave it at that, eh?"

"Then why not put it to the test?" Reeves-Galway insisted. "We can find ideal conditions here in the Scillies. Didn't you say you were sailing tonight?"

"That is my intention. The *Globe* is ready and there is a full moon with a fair breeze. Sailing by moonlight is a favourite with me in these waters."

"I shall be taking the *Dolphin* out later after the congers."

"Another test of your strength, eh? Hauling those brutes aboard."

"In a way, but not to be compared with finding oneself up against an intelligent adversary. Why not put into Samson at the end of your sail, say at 2 a.m.? I shall be there, waiting. The island is uninhabited. Then we can match wits and strength. If you think your training gives you an advantage then that will be nullified by my being there first and seeing you come ashore. I shall be stalking you, Sikes. It won't just be a question of your finding me."

"My dear chap!" Sikes protested. He was

plainly annoyed. "Hide and seek on an uninhabited island at two in the morning! For Pete's sake! What do you take me for?"

"A man who claims that his training makes him a better man than me but won't put it to the test," Reeves-Galway came back at him with an undoubted sneer.

We heard Sikes's chair screech as he pushed it back.

"I don't very much like your last remark," he said in icy tones. "I ought to ignore it but I won't. I'll meet you on Samson, Reeves-Galway, on one condition. The loser pays a hundred pounds to the local lifeboat fund. Agreed?"

"Agreed."

"No umpires?"

"That would be rather difficult to arrange at short notice, Colonel. We're both men of honour."

"OK! Thank you for your hospitality. I shall sail into Samson and go ashore in the dinghy as near to two o'clock as I can make it, bringing with me sufficient rope to tie you. At least your crazy game will have one benefactor. The local lifeboat fund will be a hundred pounds the richer. I'll be seeing you!"

The chunk of a closing door finished the taped episode. Everard raised astounded eyes to mine. He was about to speak when a woman's voice came from the still running tape.

"Victor! What has happened? You are in a terrible state. Where . . ."

"Go back to bed." Reeves-Galway's voice was a croak of exhaustion. "You know where I've been, fishing. I landed a big one. It was a hell of a fight. Go back to bed, Lola. I'll take a bath. Tell you about it later."

The tape went silent and then ran on to one of Cookson's interviews with a client. We listened for a bit but nothing more came through that had been recorded in the Scillies. Everard reached forward and switched off.

"Christ!" he exclaimed, "I can't stand anymore. The female, I take it, was Mrs. Reeves-Galway?"

"And she's a liar," I said. "She told me that she had gone back to the mainland with the boy before Sikes disappeared."

"Perhaps she did, Martin. The tape has been edited. The conversations we've heard are not necessarily recorded in chronological order. Those are Cookson's master tapes from which he would re-record separate conversations for the benefit of blackmail victims. Doubtless he thought that the husband coming home exhausted to be questioned by his wife puts a convincing touch to the agreement to meet on Samson."

He paused for a long time.

"Well, what do you make of it?" he asked wearily.

"Something I've long suspected," I answered bitterly, "only my suspicion was so outrageous I had to discard it while I sought for a saner reason. Reeves-Galway is a howling lunatic!"

He nodded doubtfully and picked up a pencil to tap it thoughtfully by its flat end on the desk.

"I wish we could prove it, Martin. Terribly difficult. I'm not sure of the value of these tapes in a court of law. But I think you're right . . ."

"Of course I'm right!" I exploded. "The man is a homicidal maniac when the mood is on him. Why, when he hired me here in London he could see me as a possible adversary in one of his moonlight duels. He killed Sikes that night on Samson. He keeps a pair of matched throwing knives on his yacht. I reckon that he took them ashore, threw one to Sikes, and told him it was a fight to the death! The colonel wouldn't have had the option with that maniac on his tail, even if he'd realised the true state of affairs and decided to beat it to the beach and his dinghy. Listen, Charles, this I think was the pattern."

I paused.

"Go on," he urged.

"Blagdon was Reeves-Galway's first victim, probably under similar circumstances . . . maybe even on Samson. That's where Reeves-Galway gets his kicks on an uninhabited island. Now Cookson introduced Blagdon to Reeves-Galway, and when the ex-cop disappeared without trace Cookson had his suspicions."

"I think it more likely that Blagdon was killed aboard his yacht," Everard interrupted. "The body was recovered from the sea. I'm sorry, Martin. Please go on."

"Cookson saw the possibility of blackmail. You've got to remember that he's a crafty number. I think he could have been digging for information about Reeves-Galway, and learnt as much as we have done, including the stay in L'Hôpital de Grise. He may even have learnt what episode it was that took Reeves-Galway there as a voluntary patient. So he went to the Scillies in April, undoubtedly following

Reeves-Galway though he told me that it was coincidence."

"Don't forget, also," Everard prompted me "that Cookson was on St. Mary's last year at the same time as Reeves-Galway but *before* Blagdon went to the Scillies."

I nodded.

"Probably the time when Reeves-Galway asked him to find a man for future employment; a man to certain specifications. Strong and active. A man with no responsibilities or near relatives, like Chester and me. Cookie, if he had guessed at Reeves-Galway's predilections by then, probably realised that Blagdon was to be a victim."

I waved a hand at the tape recorder.

"We know now that Cookie went well prepared. He heard the two men, Reeves-Galway and Sikes agree to meet in the small hours on Samson. When the news came through of the colonel's yacht drifting on to the Seven Sisters Reef, but without Sikes aboard, he *knew* what had happened. He might even have been there himself on the island . . ."

"How, Martin? Sergeant Bolt has checked on the movements of all boats in and out of harbour . . ."

"He might have stowed himself aboard the *Dolphin*. He could have done, you know. Reeves-Galway could have had her moored to the quay that night, with the covers off, ready to go. Come to think of it, Charles," I added eagerly, "Cookson *must* have been on Samson that night. Because as soon as the fuss following Sikes' disappearance had died down; the enquiries made; Cookie was over there . . . a week later as it happened. He knew exactly where Sikes was buried. He unearthed the body, photographed it and either reburied it in another spot, or took it to sea and sank it truly."

"And used the photograph to blackmail Reeves-Galway?" Everard asked. "I'm not certain I go along with that, Martin. Surely Reeves-Galway must have guessed it was Cookson who sent it?"

"Why on earth should he? You don't know Cookson. He can put on a damned good act when he wants. You've heard his voice on the tape interviewing his clients. Butter wouldn't melt in his mouth. Reeves-Galway probably considers him a charming chap; a gentleman who through force of circumstances has been compelled to follow a somewhat dubious trade.

No, Reeves-Galway has not suspected Cookson. He's not to know that his hotel room was bugged, or that Cookson has been on his tail for months, waiting like a hyena for the next kill."

I stopped as Everard's secretary came into the room after a brief knock. She was carrying a tray on which were two cups of tea.

"Thank you, Peggy," Everard smiled. "You'll never know how thankful I am to receive this particular cup, even though it has been brewed by Sergeant Knowles."

It was real Army tea, brown as old leather.

"Not too strong I hope," Peggy murmured to me. "Sugar?"

I thanked her and said that I liked all things sweet. She blushed and hurried out.

"With the photograph and the first demand note Cookson must have told Reeves-Galway that he had emptied the original grave and buried the body elsewhere. He probably threatened to produce it for the authorities or at least tell them exactly where it was buried. I think it likely that Reeves-Galway paid the first demand. He then hit on the idea of finding the second grave in the company of two witnesses having hinted to Sergeant Bolt that Sikes had been smuggling diamonds. If he found the body that way it was unlikely that the authorities would suspect him of having buried it."

"Do you think Cookson reburied it?" Everard demanded.

"I doubt it. If he did somewhere on Samson then Reeves-Galway would have found it by now. No, I think Cookson sank it at sea. He probably considered that it might prove an embarrassment to him at some stage, and he still had Reeves-Galway by the shorts. He had a photograph of the body in its grave, and he had a taped recording of the agreement to meet on Samson. He anticipated Reeves-Galway searching for it. Indeed he *knew* that he would for Reeves-Galway, not knowing that Cookson was the blackmailer, probably gave him the story of the diamond smuggling and his belief that Sikes was buried on an uninhabited island when he asked him to engage a couple of likely characters to help in the work. So Cookson employed the Sprott brothers and their mates to frighten Reeves-Galway off Samson, thus helping to heighten the fiction that the body was still there and would be produced if the next demand was not met." I paused and finished my tea. "I reckon that's about the size of it, Charles," I concluded.

He said nothing for a long while then raised haggard eyes.

"Poor Sikes!" he growled. "Can you imagine the dilemma he was in? Kill or be killed? He probably lost his life through trying to put Reeves-Galway down without actually harming the man. God! What a mess. It won't be easy, Martin. Two doctors will have to certify him."

It was not like Everard to be indecisive but I could sympathise with him. He had to deal with it officially, whereas I was free to act as I liked. I got to my feet glancing at my watch.

"They *must* pick up Cookson," he declared, "and make him talk. You off, Martin?"

"Back to the Scillies," I said. "There are two people for whom I have great regard cooped on a yacht with Reeves-Galway. I want them off it. I know its probably an old wives tale that madmen are affected by a full moon in spite of the derivation of the word lunatic, but the moon is getting near to fat, Charles. I don't want Meg within a mile of Reeves-Galway, nor Chester, who might find himself offered the same terms as Sikes. In the meantime get the wheels of officialdom turning."

I caught the nine o'clock boat from Penzance the next morning. As usual there was no seat going on the helicopter.

As the *Scillonian*, crowded with her usual load of trippers on a fine day, crept towards the quay through the froth from her own propeller in reverse, I made a lone figure against the port rail scanning the yachts and shipping in the harbour. I'd known it for some time but still I kept looking even when the gang plank was down. The *Dolphin* was not there.

13

MRS. PEPPIAT was no help. She and Annie were having a comfortable time in Coronel House while the owner and his family were living aboard the *Dolphin*.

"He said that he would either telephone or send a wire giving me the date of his return," the old lady told me. "I haven't heard anything yet, Mr. Yates. I think he's only cruising about the Islands. It's such lovely weather. Don't suppose he'll come home till it breaks. Three or four days yet I reckon. I have heard they're getting worried about the water. One of the wells is dry already."

St. Mary's draws its fresh water from wells, there being no springs or rivers on the island.

Mrs. Peppiat pressed me to stay for lunch; an invitation which I was delighted to accept. She showed no curiosity about my return, nor did she make any comment on my getting the sack. The fact that Reeves-Galway would have gnashed his teeth in rage had he known that

227

she was giving me lunch in his house didn't seem to bother her either.

Immediately after a cup of coffee I thanked the old lady and walked down to Hugh Town. For all Mrs. Peppiat was bothered I could have taken one of the cars, but I preferred the walk recalling how I had gone that way with Meg, and with Felix skipping along in front. It seemed years ago.

First, I thought, I had to get myself a boat, and then I would have to ask questions of the boatmen along the quay as to the whereabouts of the *Dolphin*. I dared not take it for granted that Reeves-Galway was still grave-searching at nights on Samson, cross to the island, and endure a fruitless night long wait if in fact the yacht was miles away. My immediate concern was to warn Meg and Chester of the true state of affairs, so that they could take themselves off the yawl to safety. Meg in particular. Chester might be able to take care of himself.

I thought of the cutter Meg had used to fish me out of the sea, but Jim Benton, her owner, was not in the telephone book. However, there were at least three names listed of men I had known when they'd been boys. Two were out, and the third, who I'm sure didn't really remember me but was far too polite to say so, suggested I tried a man named Cooper, who owned a twelve-foot sailing dinghy. Cooper ran a small radio and television repair business close to the Post Office, and was known to hire out his twelve-footer to visitors.

He was out when I called. I had to twiddle my thumbs till he returned after half an hour. He was a lean sandy-haired man with kindly eyes and a long jaw, who was a little wary till I assured him that I had sailed the waters round the Scillies for years as a boy, then he locked up his shop and took me down to the beach to show me the dinghy. He wanted ten shillings an hour, and I struck a bargain with him at ten pounds for twenty-four hours. I could ill afford it, but I had a feeling that I was going to be out for a long time in his dinghy. There was a locker in her stern with a key in it, and I stowed away the small travel bag I had brought with me, then went off to buy food and drink.

When the launches began coming back from the outer islands with the visitors they had taken out in the morning or at midday I went along the quay to ask questions of the boatmen. They all knew the *Dolphin*, but it was not until I asked the launch that had come in from St.

Martin's where she had called after a trip round the Eastern Isles that I got any joy. Both the skipper and his engineer reckoned they had seen the yawl about seven miles out north of St. Martin's. She had been in and out of the Islands all the week, and it was now common knowledge that her owner was looking for the grave of the yachtsman who disappeared last April. The *Dolphin* anchored off Samson nearly every night. So much for Reeves-Galway's fear of publicity. He was going to get a damned sight more than he'd ever bargained for, I thought grimly as I went back to the beach to get Cooper's twelve-footer into the water.

There was a fair breeze out of the south-west, but once I was clear of the harbour I let go of tiller and mainsail, so that she came up into the wind while I lugged my bag out of the locker. It was very hot with the sun reflecting from the water whose waves turned it into a hundred dancing mirrors. I was glad to change into bathing trunks and to feel the cool breeze on my sweating skin.

I had plenty of time, and I spent it sailing idly up and down the Road. The dinghy was a handy craft. She had a centre board and when this was down she could sail close to the wind.

When it was pulled up her draught was negligible. I would be able to take her right in on to any beach.

I would have enjoyed the sailing, for conditions were ideal, but for worry nagging my mind. It was Meg, and what could happen to her if Reeves-Galway went into one of his maniacal fits, that kept gnawing me. I was gone on the girl. I kept seeing her sweet face, her big serene grey eyes, and her lithe figure; wishing she was with me. The prospect was really a hopeless one, for I was no catch to any woman with about thirty pounds in the bank and another twenty or so in my wallet in the stern locker. Very little else except an income from a trust fund that just about paid the rent.

I kept an eye lifted for the *Dolphin*, though I had small hope of actually seeing her. With a yacht of her weight and sailing power Reeves-Galway, if he intended making Samson for the night, might bring her in from any point. East round St. Mary's and through the Sound, or west way out in the Atlantic to come in down the South-West Channel in the Road.

At eight o'clock when the fire had gone from the sun I ran the dinghy over to Tresco's long silver beach at Pentle Bay, dropped her tiny anchor, and went overside for a swim. The water was as clear as crystal, and I could see my own shadow moving below me across the white sandy bottom.

Back in the boat I had an alfresco meal of cold chicken, salad and rolls with butter I spread with a penknife. I washed it down with two tins of lager. Eaten after an invigorating swim, and in the open air under the brittle evening light off an island beach, the costliest meal in the world's finest hotel would not have tasted so good.

Smoking a contemplative cigarette I realised with a minor shock that the breeze was dropping. Windless nights in the Scillies are as rare as holy days in Red Russia, but they can happen and for me to be caught on Tresco with no wind would be disaster. It wouldn't worry Reeves-Galway in the diesel-powered *Dolphin* but there was not so much as a paddle aboard the dinghy. I cast anxious eyes at the burgee, which was barely fluttering. There were only a few hatfuls of wind around. I reckoned I would have to cross the tide getting to Samson, and if the breeze dropped to nothing I'd be stuck in the Road as helpless as a toad on a raft.

I scanned the beach looking for driftwood,

but its long length presented a practically virgin silver, darkening as the sun dropped behind the Abbey. On an impulse I went overside, waded ashore and began a search for a flat piece of wood or anything that might make a serviceable paddle. Why the hell had I not had the sense to sail and anchor off Samson instead of Tresco?

I found a handy piece of flat board fencing at last but I'd had to move inland along the Pool Road beside the Great Pool before I came across it, just in time, before the gathering gloom of evening had hidden it.

Back in the dinghy there was no wind at all, and the sun had gone leaving the flaming Scillonian dusk. A three-quarter moon was hanging in the eastern sky as yellow as cheese.

There was some breeze, if only a catspaw, out in the Road, I decided. Where I was, nearly on the beach, I was in the lee of Tresco. But the tide would help at least till I was in the Road. Pray God the wind didn't move more to the west, for if it did I would be heading straight into wind and tide as I made for Samson.

With the aid of the makeshift paddle, which was hell on my hands, and the tide as well, I moved slowly southwards till the dinghy was clear of Tobaccoman's Point. There was a whiff of breeze here. The mainsail bellied, held, and the dinghy gathered way enough for me to head her towards the twin peaks of Samson, then the sails flapped as limp as seaweed and she fell away. I worked with the paddle.

A shag went by only a few yards off making for its rocky home in the last of the light. It flew flat as a board about a foot above the water making an enviable fifteen knots to my half a one.

A speed boat came down the channel from New Grimsby, making a racket and sending out a bow wave that rocked me mockingly when it reached the dinghy.

The moon was bright silver now turning the water black except for a shimmering path between me and the hard white orb in the sky.

I kept getting hatfuls of wind that gave me a few yards at a time, enough to hold me against the drift of the tide, and some earnest paddling sent me forward. I kept at it and made progress but it was painfully slow. I reckoned that on the course I was taking the distance was two miles, and if I kept getting the odd cupful of wind it would take me four hours.

Suddenly it arrived in a steady even blow and

held me chuckling along for about two hundred yards, then it died as quickly as it had sprung.

I think I might have given up if I'd not seen the *Dolphin* arrive. I heard her diesel bubbling astern, and she passed me about a hundred yards to port; a ghost ship lovely in the moonlight, ghosting along at quarter speed. There were lights behind her port-holes and I fancied I could see two men in the cockpit though I couldn't recognise them as Chester and Reeves-Galway. She faded into the milky night. By the set of her bows she was going in between Stony Island and Green Island. She would find a greater depth of water than she had the night I'd been aboard her.

Two hours later, with my hands and shoulders aching as if I'd been on the rack I made Samson's beach, nipped overboard and lugged the dinghy hard and dry. I could see the *Dolphin*, anchored about a hundred yards out, and perhaps twice that distance from me. She showed no lights, and appeared absolutely still, frozen into moonlit glass.

I rested up for a bit lying flat on the sand. The air was as warm as a Mediterranean night's. Nothing stirred. Then I had something to eat, drank the last two tins of lager, finished a cigarette and felt fighting fit.

I walked along the beach till I was opposite the *Dolphin* and there was her dinghy on the sand. It meant probably that Reeves-Galway was ashore with Chester. Lola, Meg and the boy were on the *Dolphin* asleep in their bunks.

The island, colourless under the moon, showed absolutely no signs of life. The two men must be on its western side somewhere. I thought of using the dinghy but its outboard would split the still night wide apart with its noise, and I had no wish for Reeves-Galway to know that I was boarding his yacht. The idea of paddling again so soon after my earlier efforts didn't appeal to me. I slipped into the water and began wading. It would take no longer.

There was not a sound from the yacht as I hauled myself up her anchor chain to the bows. The water cascaded from me like molten silver and I seemed to be making as much noise as a hippo. I went along the deck to the cockpit, dropped down and through to the saloon where I switched on a light, then went forward towards the cabins. I hadn't a clue which one housed the girl and I called softly:

236

"Meg!" Then loudly, "Meg! Where are you?"

I heard the switch click on and then the state-room door flew open flooding the companion way with light. It was Lola in a diaphanous short nightie more exciting than nudity.

"Yeets!" she screeched. "What do you do here? What has happened?"

Her eyes were huge and scared.

"Nothing yet," I snapped. "Just paying a social call. Where is Miss Watkins?"

"She is ashore on the island with Chester and my husband."

"Still grave-searching?"

It was incredible how the idea stuck in the man's mind. Hadn't he realised by now that he was being played for a sucker? No telling how Reeves-Galway's mind, crazy at times, would view the problem, however.

Lola put out a hand. She was ready to go into her clutching act, but she pulled it back again.

"You are wet," she said huskily. "Dry yourself, eh, Yeets? They will not be back till it is light."

"No time for fun and games, Lola," I said deciding to play it brutally, for she would have to learn sometime. "You know why your husband is looking for a grave, don't you? He killed Sikes, buried him on Samson. Now he thinks that Cookson who has been blackmailing him has moved the grave."

She went white as the moon, and clutched dramatically at her breasts.

"*Mamma mia!*" she whispered. "Is not true. What are you saying?"

"It's true," I said. "Why else would he be searching, night after night?"

"No! Tonight is first time since you . . . you went away. There have been people on the island, living in tents. Is true. Tonight they have gone."

Visitors do camp on Samson. Fresh water is the problem for them. If Reeves-Galway had found a troop of boy scouts, for instance, encamped on the slopes of North Hill it would have put paid to his searching till they had gone.

"Is not true," Lola persisted, "what you say about Victor?"

"You know it's true," I answered harshly. "If you haven't guessed what happened to Sikes then you know what happened to Blagdon, the big red-headed man who called himself Phillips and helped crew the yacht at times last year."

She moaned, clutched wildly at the door jamb, missed, and was sliding to the deck when I grabbed her.

I picked her up, carried her into the saloon and stretched her out on one of the long bench seats. She looked like a statue; a beautiful one, and her eyes were as blank as stone.

I found the brandy bottle, went back to her, got her head down, and when she came round made her swig at the bottle. She coughed and sobbed wildly clinging to me like a frightened child.

"Is true," she whimpered eventually. "He is crazy man at times. Last year he fought the big man with a knife. I think, perhaps it was because of me. I . . . what is word? Encourage? *Si!* I encouraged Phillips a little. I did not think Victor was jealous, you understand? He has never been jealous, but . . ."

"Not jealousy," I said. "He wanted an excuse for a fight to the death. That's the way he's crazed. It was on the yacht?"

"*Si!* Here in the saloon. Afterwards he put chains round the feet and . . ."

I'd heard enough.

"Hold this!" I said roughly, and thrust the brandy bottle into her hands.

She wailed loudly as I went out of the saloon. All I hoped was that the kid had slept soundly through it all and had not been eavesdropping, frightened to show himself.

I went over the counter in a long shallow dive and beat it to the island. It was my guess, if North Hill had been occupied for a week, that it was there I would find Meg and Chester, stretching tapes for the search. There was no urgency really, I kept telling myself. On the other hand there was no guarantee that Reeves-Galway, officially classified by the year's understatement as having a disturbed personality, would not go off at half-cock at any moment, particularly now that he was on his favourite hunting ground, an uninhabited island and beneath a near full moon grinning at him like an accomplice.

I found the path of short turf and jog trotted along it my canvas shoes squelching loudly at every step.

I saw it a long way off, nothing but a black humpy shape in the middle of the path, not a man upright on his feet but an animal perhaps, an enormous dog. Then as I went nearer I saw

240

with horror slowing my steps that it was indeed a man, on his hands and knees, crawling towards me along the path.

It was Chester, and as I reached him he collapsed on his side and rolled over on his back. His long face was green in the moonlight and there was a trickle of black from the corner of his mouth, but his eyes were open.

"Steve!" I gasped. "It's me . . . Martin! What the hell . . . ?"

His voice bubbled, guttural from his throat. "He's mad. Made me fight with a knife. Bastard got me . . . Meg! She saw it. He's looking for her . . . Oh God!"

He went still and I gazed wildly up the moonlit slope of North Hill looking for any sort of movement. There was none. The rock on the summit was whitish under the moon, and the bracken growing in serried ranks below a glistening grey. There was not a sight of Reeves-Galway or Meg.

14

"LOLA!" I bawled, as I went alongside the *Dolphin*, "Lola!" She'd heard the dinghy's motor and came scrambling into the cockpit pulling a black jersey over her head and down over the top of her pants.

I'd managed to get Chester, carrying him in a fireman's lift, as far as the dinghy to bring him alongside the yacht. He was alive and that was all I knew except that the knife tip must have punctured his lung.

Together we got him aboard, and I took him through the saloon and into a bunk. Lola was weeping. I gripped her shoulders and shook her till her head rocked.

"Listen, Lola. You've got to do this on your own. Chester must be taken to hospital. You're going to sail the yacht across to St. Mary's. You can do it. When you get there tie up at the quay by the steps then yell for help. Come on. I'll hoist the anchor for you."

I pushed her towards the cockpit. She knew as much about the yawl as anyone. She had the diesel rumbling before I had the anchor inboard and stowed. The yacht was moving forward as I jumped into the dinghy and unhitched. Young Felix had awakened and come through to the cockpit. His face scared and chalk white in the moonlight was the last thing I saw as the dinghy swung in the wake of the yacht, and I tugged on the starting cord.

I sent the dinghy careering diagonally northwards towards the spot where I had beached Cooper's twelve-footer. Cookson's gun was in the bottom of my travel bag in the stern locker. It was a Magnum, and I needed it. If Reeves-Galway had harmed Meg in any way he was going to get a bullet in almost the identical spot that he had put his knife into Chester, only he'd missed the heart, and I wouldn't.

The bastard was waiting for me. He'd heard the dinghy's motor, of course, and guessed its import. I shut off the Evinrude and coasted in to the beach. Behind me the *Dolphin*'s diesel beat loudly in the still air. Good for Lola. She had the yawl on full throttle.

He was standing in the King of the Castle attitude I remembered. Legs wide apart. No jacket, just a white shirt, smeared dirty in places, and narrow flannels. A hand resting on the hilt of a knife stuck in his waist band.

He grinned when he saw me.

"Yates!" he exclaimed almost with relish. "I might have guessed it. You've found Chester. He was a poor adversary. I'm sure you'll prove better."

I've read somewhere that you are supposed to humour madmen. It occurred to me then. Not this one, I thought. He's not crazy enough. But he was standing too close to the twelve-footer. He'd be on me before I could open the locker.

The dinghy grounded and I hopped out to stand in the water. I never took my eyes off him at all. Not for a split second.

"Where's the girl?" I demanded.

He laughed. If anything betrayed his madness it was his laugh. High-pitched and cackling like a demented rooster's.

"She was good," he said. "She could run like a deer, and fight too! She had more guts than Chester. But, of course, she couldn't beat me. Your turn to try, Yates. You, I think should prove the most able of the lot. I'm sorry I can't let you have a knife. The other was lost. But I'll give you fifty yards start. Come ashore, Yates."

244

I scarcely heard his last words. When he mentioned Meg the moon could have toppled out of the sky and I wouldn't have noticed. It was as if the world had come to an end for me. I'd been concerned to save Chester's life, praying to God that Meg could elude this madman long enough for me to get back from the yacht. I didn't really care that Reeves-Galway had murdered and murdered again. I could find no sorrow for what might happen to his family when the truth came out. I was not even in that rare moment concerned for myself.

A terrible anger flooded me, and I gritted my teeth. I was about to rush him when ten yards behind him where the bracken grew Meg rose into sight like a vision. She was in her shorts and a jersey. Her clothing was almost white in the moonlight. Her long tanned legs as dark as pewter.

I swore at myself under my breath in relief. I'd nearly fallen for it. I ought to have known that Reeves-Galway would never admit defeat by a girl, or even that he had been unable to catch her. Meg was no ghost. She had followed him down to the beach, keeping her distance and herself out of sight.

"Don't be afraid, Yates," Reeves-Galway

said. "Come ashore. I've promised you fifty yards start."

"Not I. Not this time, you bloody maniac," I retorted. "I'm staying in the water. What makes you think you're so good?" I taunted him. "You only beat Sikes and Chester because they daren't knife you back. They'd have been in trouble if they had. They couldn't believe you were a daftie. I know better. You're a crazy man—as crazy as a coot. I'm staying here."

"You've signed your own death warrant, Yates. I offered you fifty yards start. Now you'll die."

He whipped the knife out of his waistband, and came charging through the water at me. I stepped backwards, watching him. He could probably throw the knife with some skill. That was the danger. If I could get him out to deeper water where it was up to our necks he would be hampered in making a thrust. He could only hold the knife high and strike downwards; a stroke which I could easily counter.

The sea bottom was sandy. There was some weed, but not enough to delay one. The real menace were small rocks below the surface. Moving backwards I could put a foot on one, and tip myself into the water before I was ready to swim.

He waded steadily after me, and because he was moving forwards and I backwards he was narrowing the gap between us. I kept taunting him, because I didn't want him to realise that the deeper the water the less the advantage from the knife, or to have an inkling of my real intention.

But Reeves-Galway's madness was only in his obsession that he was a superb fighter, and presumably that he could put it to the test with impunity whenever he could inveigle a likely opponent to meet him in a suitable spot. The sea was not such a place.

"All right, Yates!" he snarled. "I don't fight cowards. I'll wait for you on shore. You'll change your mind before long. Besides, I never caught the girl. She's better sport than you."

He turned and began wading back. I put my wet hands to my mouth and bawled:

"Meg! My bag in the stern locker of the twelve-footer. There's a gun in it!"

She caught on in an instant. I saw her pale shadowy figure dart towards the sailing dinghy.

Reeves-Galway saw her too, but he was hampered by the water up to his waist. So was

I as I charged after him. I saw him stumble and fall, but he picked himself up in a moment. Meg was in the dinghy bending over the locker.

The water grew shallower, and Reeves-Galway could run. The water spewed upwards from his pumping legs showering outwards like a fountain of silver. I followed. I doubted that he could hear me above his own noisy splashing.

The beached sailing dinghy was only six feet from the water's edge, and I could see Meg clearly. She was obviously fumbling in the bag. Then she stood up. I couldn't see the gun in her hand with the moon over her shoulder, and nor did I look very hard, for Reeves-Galway came to an abrupt halt. His right arm came back and jerked forward. The knife glinted for an instant in the moonlight as it sped arrow straight towards the beached boat. Then I was on him with my forearm round his neck against his throat, my knee in his back and heaving with all my strength.

The man was incredibly strong. I had noted before his great width of shoulder, and now I realised jammed up against him that this width made him appear stocky. He was in fact nearly as tall as I was. His flesh was rock hard beneath the thin shirt. In an instant utter dismay flooded my whole being. That he was mad was bad enough, but this sudden discovery of his physical qualities, his vast width of muscled shoulder and iron back, turned him into a monster.

I couldn't hold him. He bent forward with the greatest of ease and flung me over his head. I went flat in the eighteen inches of water, and Meg fired the gun. She told me afterwards that it was half an accident; that it was the first clear view she'd had of Reeves-Galway and that she'd squeezed it in pure surprise. She'd never fired a pistol in her life before and the bullet went God knows where.

I heard it, realised that the knife must have missed her and took some heart from the thought. I needed it.

I'd twisted over in the water immediately I hit it. Pure instinct demanded that I never present my back to Reeves-Galway for half a second. He was lunging down on me. I lifted a foot and kicked him in the groin. That checked him long enough for me to find a footing. He came in again and I tried a judo throw. It was a mistake, wet hands trying to grip wet flesh. He jolted me with a body punch, but he was too close. I stood off and belted him a quick one two to the jaw. It was like hitting the side of a house. The light was tricky and the sandy footing shifted as I struck. This was no good, I decided. I wanted him in deep water, but would he follow?

I circled warily. He had his two hands held out, crooked like talons in front of him. If he was going for my throat he was telegraphing it.

I backed away seawards, and he laughed his crazy cackle. As if to remind him what awaited him if he decided to leave me and go ashore Meg loosed off another shot with the Magnum. It was no more accurate than the first had been, but it decided Reeves-Galway. He came after me.

With the water up to my waist I turned and struck out in a fast crawl. After fifty yards I trod water looking for him. The bastard was after me, arms flashing, coming through the water like a torpedo.

I could still touch bottom. Another fifty yards and the depth was right. I stayed still legs idling. He had lagged somewhat and his stroke was laboured. That suited me. I dived from the surface, went to the bottom and swam towards him. I could see the shadow of his wide body through the green silvery light of the moonlit water, detect his hands pulling through the water like paddles.

I kicked off the bottom and grabbed him, kneed him in the stomach, let him go and shot to the surface for air. He came up alongside me. I'd surprised him all right and my knee to his stomach, weakened as the blow had been through the hampering water, had been enough to drive the wind out of him. He was not concerned for my whereabouts. All he needed was air. He dragged some down, making a queer screeching noise before I was on him again; on his shoulders, driving him down and down through the darkening water, riding him like Sinbad's old man of the sea. I had been ready for the move and he had not.

His body threshed and jerked. We rolled in the water but still I gripped him with arms and legs, and stayed there till the blood was roaring in my own ears like the sound of an express train. This was the final moment, I knew. There would never be another chance. He had to die if I died with him.

I felt him go limp. I let go, kicked to the surface, expelled used air, gulped in fresh, and went down again. He might have been foxing.

But he wasn't. His body was there, a strange amorphous lump by the weird light of the moon through the water, rolling gently in the tide.

I left it, rose to the surface, and swam slowly shorewards. Meg had waded out to meet me, the gun held high out of the water.

"Oh, Martin!" was all she said, and the tone of her voice told me all I wanted to know.

We waded ashore with my arm round her. She was shivering.

I thought of getting over to St. Mary's straight away. We could have made it in the dinghy with the twelve-footer in tow, but after resting up for a bit I decided it would be prudent to stay.

A police launch came in at dawn, and by then my story was ready. Reeves-Galway and his party had arrived on Samson where I had become immobilised in the sailing dinghy. I'd kept out of their way because a week previously I had been sacked from his employ. I had seen the party come ashore but I had avoided them. Later, when I had realised that I would have to spend the night on the island I'd gone looking for a likely spot in which to bed down, and come across Chester crawling towards the beach. I had got him aboard the *Dolphin*, and then, anxious about the girl, had returned to the beach because Chester had managed to tell me that his boss must have had a brainstorm. Reeves-Galway had been waiting for me and attacked me with a knife. To elude him I'd swum out to sea. I had heard him in the water behind me and swum on desperately, but when I'd trod water to look round to see if he was still in pursuit I had failed to spot him. I had swum cautiously back to shore and found Meg there, who had told me she had seen Reeves-Galway go under. Together we had swum out to look for him but had failed to find him.

I'm sure the story was not entirely believed; certainly not by Sergeant Bolt when it reached him. But it was supported in every detail by Meg, who had worked it out with me anyway. Since there were no other witnesses and I had taken care to find the two empty rounds she had loosed off from the Magnum they had no option but to accept it. I signed a statement.

As soon as we were landed on St. Mary's we went straight to the hospital. Chester was still alive and the doctor was hopeful.

Then I thought of Lola, and we went on to Coronel House.

I think she had guessed what had happened.

She was still in her black jersey and pants, and the flesh round her wide eyes was as dark as her garb.

"He drowned," I said simply. I couldn't bring myself to recite the fiction that Meg and I had swum out to look for him.

Lola went into paroxysms of grief, but I had the feeling that she felt it was expected of her rather than the true emotions of a girl tragically widowed.

Meg and I explained as best we could what would happen; that when Reeves-Galway's body was found there would be an inquest.

I pointed out that the fact that Chester had been attacked and nearly killed would bring to light her husband's periodical attacks of madness. There was no concealing them. She had already told me what had happened to Blagdon, and I could see no sense in dragging that into a coroner's court. She agreed.

"But," I said, "if you can help with the death of Colonel Sikes, Lola, then I think you should. His body has not been found and that presents certain legal difficulties about the presumption of his death and the administration of his estate."

254

I doubt if she understood half of what I said. She shook her head.

"I was not in the hotel, Yeets, that night. I told you."

Early as it was, Mrs. Peppiat was up. She brought in tea, and offered us breakfast later. Meg went up to her own room, and to look in on the boy, whom she regarded as her charge still. I drank a cup of tea, uncomfortable in Lola's presence, and was thinking of leaving when she said:

"Victor wrote in a book at times. It is in his desk but I have not the keys. They are on the *Dolphin*. If you will fetch them, Yeets, I will look."

"You mean he kept a diary?" I asked.

"*Si*, that is the word. A diary. It was very secret."

I went out to the garage, started up the Morris, and buzzed it down to the quay. The *Dolphin* was still tied there. The launch that had fetched us from Samson had towed the dinghy and the twelve-footer astern. Somebody had already hitched the dinghy to the *Dolphin*.

Within ten minutes I had found Reeves-Galway's keys in the state room and was back at Coronel House unlocking his desk.

The diary was a big day-to-a-page volume handsomely bound in blue leather. Under the 28th April he had written in a big sprawling script, which alone is supposed to be a sign of mental instability, the following:

Tonight Colonel Sikes accepted my challenge. I was infinitely excited and nearly frantic with worry that he would change his mind, because I believe him to be a coward. I had a black-out when I saw his yacht creeping into the island to anchor offshore. I was sure that he would prove a dangerous adversary once he had been brought to the fight, and I suppose the excitement and strain of waiting was too much for me. However, I recovered before he was ashore. He was comically shaken when I threw him a knife and he retreated to the beach, or would have done had I not cut him off. He fought well, once he had realised that there was no other way. He had me at his mercy once when I slipped and fell but for some reason he stood off to give me another chance.

I stopped reading at that point. Up till then, particularly in Lola's presence, I had been experiencing a certain feeling of guilt in the way I had let Reeves-Galway drown. I could have towed his body ashore and perhaps brought him round by artificial respiration, when the madness would have been washed out of him. But after reading his failure to recognise Sikes' action in not knifing him after he had slipped for what it was, then I realised that there never would have been any hope for Reeves-Galway.

The writing went on to record a fatal thrust, which it described as classic, under the fifth rib.

I buried him on Samson because I thought there was less chance of the body coming to light than if I took it to sea, *the account concluded*. I towed his yacht away behind the *Dolphin*. The wind was in the west and I set her adrift shortly before dawn so that she would fetch up on the Seven Sisters Reef. It was a safe assumption that she would break up and conceal the fact that I had lashed the tiller in order to stop her coming into the wind.

On the next day he had written:

I feel a new man. My depression has lifted miraculously after last night's success.

I leafed through the diary, but there was nothing more recorded that was not an innocent account of day to day happenings.

I handed the book to Lola.

"The police should see this," I told her, and she nodded listlessly.

"I do not care, Yeets. I will go back to Italy soon, when I am allowed."

Three days later two fishermen brought in Reeves-Galway's body. There was nothing about it to suggest that the man had died in any other way but drowning, and that was the verdict reached by the coroner's jury.

Chester's statement and Meg's evidence attracted widespread publicity. Newspaper men haunted the Islands for days.

Chester, that tough hombre, mended well. He and I are going to start a boat-building business when we can scrape up enough capital.

Lola, as she had promised went home to Italy, leaving Felix in Meg's care. This looks like becoming a permanent arrangement and the lawyers are working on it now.

Everard was satisfied that the photograph of Sikes in his grave and the production of Reeves-Galway's diary would be enough to get him official presumption of the colonel's death, but when Cookson was arrested in Waterford, Eire, and extradited, the picture was complete—for Cookie, by some means known only to Everard, was persuaded to talk. As I had guessed he had actually stowed away on the *Dolphin* in the forepeak the night Sikes had died. Cookson had watched the fight on shore from the deck of the yawl. He had been too terrified to do anything, and afterwards had endured another trip in the forepeak when Reeves-Galway had towed away Sikes' yacht. Cookie had not even had the advantage of leaving the *Dolphin* where he had joined her, at the quay, for Reeves-Galway had tied up at his mooring and Cookson had been forced to swim and wade to the beach.

Meg never talks about her experience on Samson when she saw Chester forced to fight, go down, and was then compelled to run for her life, to hide and crawl in the bracken with a madman at her heels. She openly declared again and again that she would never set foot on Samson after that night. But she did, with me one hot night in late August. We took a tent but we never used it. After all they call Samson the Honeymoon Island.

THE END

A GENTEEL LITTLE MURDER
by Philip Daniels

Gilbert had a long-cherished plan to murder his wife. When the polished Edward entered the scene Gilbert's attitude was suddenly changed.

DEATH AT THE WEDDING
by Madelaine Duke

Dr. Norah North's search for a killer takes her from a wedding to a private hospital. She deals with the nastiest kind of criminal—the blackmailer and rapist!

MURDER FIRST CLASS
by Ron Ellis

A new type of criminal announces his intention of personally restoring the death penalty in England. Will Detective Chief Inspector Glass find the Post Office robbers before the Executioner gets to them?

LITTLE DROPS OF BLOOD
by Bill Knox

It might have been just another unfortunate road accident but a few little drops of blood pointed to murder—and plunged Chief Inspector Colin Thane and Inspector Phil Moss into another adventure.

GOSSIP TO THE GRAVE
by Jonathan Burke

Jenny Clark invented Simon Sherborne because her daily gossip column was getting dull. But when the society editor demanded a picture of the elusive playboy, Jenny knew she had to get rid of him. Then Simon appeared at a party—in the flesh! And Jenny finds herself involved in murder.

HARRIET FAREWELL
by Margaret Erskine

Wealthy Theodore Buckler had planned a magnificent Guy Fawkes Day celebration. He hadn't planned on murder.

A FOOT IN THE GRAVE
by Bruce Marshall

About to be imprisoned and tortured for the death of his wife in Buenos Aires, John Smith escapes, only to become involved in an aeroplane hi-jacking.

DEAD TROUBLE
by Martin Carroll

A little matter of trespassing brought Jennifer Denning more than she bargained for. She was totally unprepared and ill-equipped for the violence which was to lie in her path.

HOURS TO KILL
by Ursula Curtiss

Margaret went to New Mexico to look after her sick sister's rented house and felt a sharp edge of fear when the absent landlady arrived. Her fears deepened into panic after she found the bloodstains on the porch.

THE DEATH OF ABBE DIDIER
by Richard Grayson
Inspector Gautier of the Sûreté investigates three crimes which are strangely connected —the murder of a vicar, the theft of a diamond necklace and the murder of Pontana's valet.

NIGHTMARE TIME
by Hugh Pentecost
Have the missing major and his wife met with foul play somewhere in the Beaumont Hotel, or is their disappearance a carefully planned step in an act of treason?

BLOOD WILL OUT
by Margaret Carr
Why was the manor house so oddly familiar to Elinor Howard? Who would have guessed that a Sunday School outing could lead to murder?

THE DRACULA MURDERS
by Philip Daniels
The Horror Ball was interrupted by a spectral figure who warned the merrymakers they were tampering with the unknown. Then a girl was ritualistically murdered on the golf course.

THE LADIES OF LAMBTON GREEN
by Liza Shepherd
Why did murdered Robin Colquhoun's picture pose such a threat to the ladies of Lambton Green?

CARNABY AND THE GAOLBREAKERS
by Peter N. Walker
Detective Sergeant James Aloysius Carnaby-King is sent to prison as bait. When he joins in an escape he is thrown headfirst into a vicious murder hunt.

VICIOUS CIRCLE
by Alan Evans
Crawford finds himself on the run and hunted in a strange land, wanting only to find his son but prepared to pay any cost.

MUD IN HIS EYE
by Gerald Hammond
The harbourmaster's body is found mangled beneath Major Smyle's yacht. What is the sinister significance of the illicit oysters?

THE SCAVENGERS
by Bill Knox
Among the masses of struggling fish in the *Tecta*'s nets was a larger, darker, ominously motionless form . . . the body of a skin diver.

DEATH IN ARCADY
by Stella Phillips
Detective Inspector Matthew Furnival works unofficially with the local police when a brutal murder takes place in a caravan camp.